In Love With the King of Chicago

By: A.J Dix

Copyright © 2017

Published by Urban Chapters Publications

www.urbanchapterspublications.com

Contains explicit languages and adult themes

suitable for ages 16+

TEXT UCP TO 22828 TO SUBSCRIBE TO OUR

MAILING LIST

If you would like to join our team, submit the first

3-4 chapters of your completed manuscript to

Submissions@UrbanChapterspublications.com

Author Notes:

Thank you for taking the time to download and read the beginning of Dez, Karter, Melodee, and Dame. I fell in love with characters, and I hope you do too. If not, just bear with me while I get it together!

I also want to thank the lovely Jahquel for believing in my writing skills, and giving me the opportunity to get my work out, and always coming with the Lil Uzi GIFs.

Brii and Dee Ann! Thank you for constantly encouraging me, and giving me great advice when I'm lost. I appreciate both of you!

Last, but definitely not least, I have to give thanks to my wonderful husband. He pushed me every day to get my writing done, even when I was tired. I had so many late nights and early mornings working on this, and he didn't complain...that much. But, I'm happy it's completed. Enjoy, and don't forget to leave a review! :)

-AJ

Contact info

I can be reached on Facebook @ AJ Dix

And don't forget to follow my Facebook reading group @ 'AJ's Reading Group' for sneak peaks and release dates for my upcoming releases!

Prologue

When you love someone, you find yourself doing things you never thought you'd do. That was definitely the case for me right now, as I stared down at person whose life I just took, or at least I think he was dead.

"Karter, come on, we gotta go."

"Did I...did I kill 'im?"

"It was either them or me, baby, but we can't sit here and discuss this shit right now."

My ears were still ringing from the gunshot, and my head was spinning. I just knew I was going to pass out, until Dez grabbed my arm and had to basically dragging me to the car. I was still holding the smoking gun as Dez drove like a bat outta hell. I didn't think I would get that visual out of my head of that body hitting the ground. I never even shot a gun before. *God, I hope I don't get punished for this.*

"Shit!"

"What?"

I snapped out of my trance to see blue lights flashing behind us. I started to panic, but Dez took the gun and stashed it in a secret compartment that was in the dash.

"Just relax, bae, I'll take care of this, it's probably because I was speeding."

I saw his lips moving, but I couldn't hear anything over the sound of my racing heart.

Dez rolled the window down halfway as one officer came to his window, and another was on the passenger side flashing his light in my face.

"License, registration, and proof of insurance, please?"

"What am I being stopped for, Officer?"

"You were going 80 in a 65, sir."

"Aite bro, I gotta reach in the glove compartment."

"Move slowly." The officer had his hand on his gun, and my eyes got big as I watched his every move. With all the shit going on with police killing black people, males especially, I feared for Dez's life as well as my own.

Dez handed over his documents, and the officers walked back to their car. Five minutes later, another squad car pulled up, and Dez cursed under his breath as they approached the car again. This time, the officer tapped on my window.

"Ma'am, do you have identification?"

"What you need her shit for? I'm the one driving, you pulled me over for speeding, right? Fuck outta here with that shit."

"Babe, it's ok, calm down." I got my license and handed it to the officer. He stepped back and said something into his walkie talkie before he came back to my window.

"Ma'am, I need you to step out and put your hands behind your back."

"Karter, don't get yo ass out this car." Dez rolled my window back up and the officer snatched at the door handle. I didn't know what to do as I felt the urge to throw up all over the place.

"You bet not fuck my door up while you snatching on my shit." The officer put his hand on his gun, but this time, he pulled it out and had it pointing at me.

"Open the door and step out, NOW!"

"Get your fucking gun out my wife face, bitch." Dez hopped out the car and sprinted around the car, and I got out too so I could stop him from doing something crazy.

"Dezmund, NO! Get back in the car, please, just get back in the car." The officer grabbed my arm and threw me against the car, and the next thing I knew, Dez punched him in the face and he hit the ground. Another squad car pulled up, and I tried to grab my phone off the seat so I could call Melodee or Dame, or anybody.

"PUT YOUR HANDS UP, NOW!"

We now had five guns drawn on us, and Dez just gave me a hug and kissed me on the lips.

"Don't say shit, whatever they ask you, ok? You. Don't. Know. Shit." Dez put his hands up and got down on his knees, so I did the same thing.

He was tackled first and put into handcuffs, then me. As I was put into the back of a police car, I cried my eyes out. Just last year, I was living a normal life and trying to make the best of it. But, ever since I fell in love with the king of Chicago, my life had been everything but normal. Just keep reading, you'll see what I mean. I'm going to rewind the last nine months.

Karter

Boom!

Boom!

"Karter, come on! You know that line is going to be super long!"

My best friend, Melodee, was banging on my door as I examined the outfit she picked for me to wear tonight.

"I feel naked, Mel, I can't wear this." I opened my room door and showed her what I looked like. I pulled at the bottom of my, dress and she popped my hand.

"Girl, it's a mini dress, you're supposed to feel naked."

"My ass cheeks are hanging out! Big Mama is probably rolling over in her grave right now."

"Naw, Big Mama is probably up there hoping you get some tonight so you can loosen up."

"Melodee!"

"What? Shit, it's the truth. All you do is go to the studio, then come home to read on that damn tablet. Tonight, you gotta let loose, and not with those thick ass glasses on."

"How am I going to freaking see, Melodee?"

"You don't need to see to have fun, shit."

"You're so irra, I swear. I'll put my contacts in."

I went into the adjoining bathroom in my room and put my contacts in. I gave myself a once over in the full-length mirror again, shut the light off, and walked out.

"Much better, bestie! Now, let's go before you try to change your mind."

We got into Melodee's car and headed to *Club Promise*. It was a new nightclub that opened a few months ago on Ontario Street. From what we heard around town, the club had the best music, food, and drinks, compared to the other local clubs.

"See, look at this line, messing with you. Huuuh."

"I thought your cousin could get us in?"

"I mean, he can if he's at the door."

"Oh my God, Melodee, I knew I should've stayed home! You got me wearing these high heels, knowing I can barely walk in them, AND I have to stand outside?"

"Stop complaining, Kay. I promise we gon' turn up."

She pulled up front so valet could park her car, and I fixed my dress before we walked to the door.

"Look, there go Rich right there. Ain't no lines, biihhh! Hey, Rich. This my girl, Karter. Karter, this is my cousin, Rich."

"Nice to meet you, shorty, you got your IDs?"

"Really, Rich? You know how old I am."

"Show me a damn ID so you can get out my face, Melodee."

I showed him my ID, and he stamped our hands.

"Yaaasss, this my song!"

Melodee was dancing all the way to the bar as "*It's a Vibe*" played through the speakers of the club.

"Hey! What can I get you two ladies?" the bartender asked as she was making another drink.

"Long Island iced tea."

"Karter, grow up, you're not drinking that shit tonight. We're going to start with six shots of Patrón."

"Coming right up."

The shots were lined up in front of us; Melodee gave me three, and she took three."

"Cheers to the fucking weekend."

I took my shots and felt like my entire body was on fire, whereas Melodee was ordering four more shots.

This girl is trying to kill me.

"These are for you, happy birthday!"

"My birthday is in September."

"Take the shots so we can try to find a table, damn Karter, you ruin everything."

I took the other four Patrón shots and followed Melodee to a table in the corner. The alcohol was starting to take over, and I was dancing in my seat while Melodee was standing up dancing.

"Let's go to the dance floor, I think I see Rodney over there."

"Please don't show your ass out here."

Rodney was Melodee's ex-boyfriend; they had been broken up for almost a year, but every time they saw each other, it was some drama.

"I'm not, come on, I just want him to see what he lost out on."

We were in the middle of the dance floor, dancing and having a good time when Rodney walked up and snatched Melodee by her arm.

"Get yo fucking hands off me."

"Let me talk to you, Mel."

"Hell no, you can move around, though."

"You good over here, cuz?" Rich popped up outta nowhere, and Rodney backed away with his hands in the air and disappeared into the crowd.

"Yeah, we ok, good looking out."

"Mel, I need to go to the bathroom; those shots are running through me."

There were about fifteen other women in the line for the bathroom, and I didn't know if I was going to make it. I started doing a little dance to get my mind off my bladder, when I saw Mel's cousin walk by.

"Hey, Rich! Is there another bathroom? I don't think I can hold it anymore."

"There's an office on the second floor. Y'all can go up there, the owner ain't here yet; just don't touch shit." He looked directly at Melodee when he said the last part, and she rolled her eyes at him.

Me and Melodee rushed up the stairs, and I ran right through the first doors I could find, hoping it was the right office.

"Girl, this office lavish as fuck!" Melodee called out as I was emptying my bladder.

"I hope you not touching nothing out there, Mel, you know you nosey as— what the fuck, Melodee, get off the computer!"

"I was just checking the camera, making sure the coast was clear; you ready to go?"

"I swear, you worse than a little kid sometimes, bring yo ass on."

I opened the door and was met with a gun pointing in my face

"Who the fuck let y'all up here?"

I kept opening and closing my mouth, trying to find my words, but I couldn't. I felt like I was about to piss on myself and I just left the bathroom.

The man in front of me put his gun down, and I finally let go of the breath I didn't know I was holding.

"Our fault, my girl couldn't hold her bladder anymore, y'all should look into getting another bathroom down there. Excuse us." Melodee grabbed my hand and tried to rush past them, but one of them grabbed my arm.

"What's your name?"

"Karter?" Before I could answer, someone called my name and I turned to see who it was. I saw Destini, a girl I went to school with, walking toward us.

"Hey, Destini girl! I ain't seen you in a minute." Melodee pushed me out the way and gave Destini a hug. We all had some classes together, but nobody saw her since junior year; her ass just disappeared.

"I know, right? How y'all been?"

"Good, until he tried to shoot Karter."

"Let me apologize for my brother, he got a thing about his personal space. Let me formally introduce everybody. Dame and Dez, Melodee and Karter, bam. Y'all come up to my section and party with me, I got unlimited bottles."

"You better be paying for that shit," Dame interrupted Destini.

"Man, mind yo bidness, y'all can just follow me. I was coming to get them, but forget it."

I walked off with Melodee and felt eyes on me. I turned around, and Dez was staring intensely at me before he walked into his office.

"Mel, I really hope you didn't take anything, I'm scared as hell."

"Girl relax, they ain't even have shit in there."

Melodee was that person that stuffed her purse with whatever she could when she was in the hospital. Shit, I had to pat her down when she left my room; you never know with her. We went to the section, and Destini introduced us to her girlfriend.

"Nice to meet you, Tiffany."

"Y'all drink Hennessy, right?"

"Hell yeah, po' up!"

She handed me a cup with some Hennessy and cranberry juice, and I took one sip and put it on the table. I was about to be sloppy drunk messing with her ass.

After the year I had, I think I deserved to get drunk and forget about my worries, but no matter the amount of liquor, Big Mama was on my mind. I'm happy she's not suffering anymore, but I missed her so much.

"Stop babysitting, Karter." Destini was turning up as the DJ was playing G Herbo's *"I Like."*

"I'm not babysitting, shut up." I took another sip of my cup and felt a chill go through my body. I couldn't tell if it was actually juice in this cup.

"Destini, where did you go senior year?"

"Shit, we moved to the suburbs, so I went to school out there... shit was weak as fuck. All them hoes wanted to be gay, until it was time to eat some pussy."

"Ewww, ok bye, cuz you tripping."

"My bad." She laughed and got up to sit by Tiffany. Destini had always been the type to say whatever she wanted, and she got in trouble so much in school because of it.

As I sat waiting for Dez to come back, I started feeling nervous. I don't know why, but something about his presence was intimidating. I probably needed to finish this whole cup before he came down here.

Dezmund "Dez"

I sat in my chair behind my oak desk, rolling my Backwood and nodding to the music the DJ was playing. Opening this club proved to be a good move for me and my brother, and it was legal, so that was definitely a plus.

I took a long pull and watched the cameras that were all over the club. I found Karter on the screen and watched as she was sipping her drink and dancing seductively in her seat. The way that burgundy dress she was wearing hugging her curves, it looked painted on.

"What you over here staring at? Aw yeah, shorty and her friend bad. I think she outta yo league, she look like a good girl."

"Fuck you tryna say, Dame?"

"Shiiiit, I dun said it already."

"Yo ass a hater. Don't worry about how I'mma handle her, you worry about that thieving ass friend of hers. Her ass was all in my drawers and shit."

"I'm fucking with you, bro. Hurry yo ass up, though. I ain't about to be in this bitch all night, either."

"Man, I'm checking profit, and I gotta order some more liquor."

"That's what the damn manager for. Why you hire the bitch if you don't trust her?"

"Because this our shit at the end of the day. If my name on something, it's gon' be right. We need another bartender, Kim look like she in the weeds down there."

"Well, roll ya sleeves up and go help her, boss man."

"Hell naw, I ain't doing shit tonight."

"Aw yeah, I know you gon' be sniffing behind lil' trespassing Karter."

"Fuck out my office, you ain't shit." I stood up and put my blunt out.

We walked out, and I made sure I locked the door behind us this time. As I made my way down the stairs to the main floor, I was being stopped by a bunch of people from my old neighborhood.

"Yo Dez, this shit bussing!"

"Good looking, bro, thanks for coming out."

I made my way to our personal section, and Dame was already booed up with Melodee. He was talking shit about me, and he flew his ass over there.

I slid into the booth next to Karter, and she gave me a nervous smile.

"You ain't gotta be scared, ma. My fault about earlier, it was just instinct."

"It's fine, I guess I should've just stayed in the line."

"So, what brings you to my establishment tonight?"

"I was kind of forced to come out, but I'm glad I did. I like it here."

"I'm glad you came out too, or we wouldn't have met… even if you were trespassing in my office."

"I'm soooo sorry. I usually wouldn't have done that, but shit, it was an emergency. I promise, we didn't touch anything."

"You good, I'm joking with you."

"Kay, you want to go to White Palace?" Her friend came interrupting us.

"Yeah, right now?"

"Yeah, unless you want to wait. Dame said he down, what about you?" she asked, looking at me.

"Yeah, I'll slide through, we can meet y'all there."

"We?"

"Yeah, Karter gon' ride with me."

"Mmhhmm. Don't make me have to come find you. Text me when you move around, Kay bay?" She switched off with Dame, Destini, and Destini's girlfriend, Tiffany.

Melodee and Karter were like polar opposites. Melodee seemed like the loud, unfiltered friend while Karter was the quiet and timid one.

"You don't look comfortable."

"It's not that. I'm just not used to this type of scene."

"Aite, I gotta go grab my shit from upstairs, then we can go."

I stood up and extended my hand out to help her up. We were walking through the crowd, and people started making a path for us to walk. Karter seemed to be shying away from the attention we were getting, but I was used to being watched. I had been running these Chicago streets since I was nine and my Pops died. I had to help take care of my family. Now, twenty years later, I finally walked away from the shit, alive and with my brother.

I grabbed my keys and suit jacket and knocked on my manager's office to let her know I was gone for the night.

"Yo Mimi, I'm out; if you need something, hit my line."

"Can you come in really quick? I need to go over something with you." She pranced to the door and stopped when she saw Karter standing behind me.

"Tell me tomorrow, just worry about shit going how it's supposed to tonight."

"Aw ok, that's fine."

She rolled her eyes and looked Karter up and down. Mimi called herself liking me, but I already told her I didn't fuck with people on my payroll. Besides, she had too many damn baby daddies for me. The kids was cool, but all six of they asses had a different father.

"You know me or something?"

"Little girl, bye."

"Nah, little boy, speak your mind. You eyeing me like you know me, so wassup?" Karter tried to step around me, and I pulled her away from the office and out the back door.

"Damn, I thought yo ass was sweet. You was about to turn into the Incredible Hulk in there."

"I am sweet, I'm just not a punk. She was rolling her eyes and staring me down like she wanted something, so I was gon' help her find it."

"You funny as hell. I see it's more to Karter than what meets the eye."

"I guess you'll just have to find out, Dez."

I helped her into the passenger seat of my car and walked around to get in.

"Sooo, what made you decide to open a club?"

"I used to party a lot. I know what type of shit appeals to a young nigga."

"Like what?"

"Bitches, music, and alcohol."

"Wow."

"I'm just being honest, baby, you gotta get used to honesty."

"Get used to it?"

"Yeah, if you gon' be around me, just know I only speak facts, and I don't talk just to hear myself speak."

"And, who are you supposed to be?"

"I ain't SUPPOSED to be shit, everybody know exactly who I am."

"And who is that?"

"Dezmund Wright, the king of the Chi, baby girl. You tryna be my queen?"

"We'll see how I feel when I'm not tipsy." I laughed, and she did too.

We pulled up, and I helped her out of the car and into the restaurant. I got a better look at her body with the extra light, and I was impressed. She was petite, but had a nice little booty. I saw a lot of potential in Miss Karter.

Melodee

"Damn, it took y'all long enough. I was about to put an APB out on yo ass."

Karter and Dez had just made it to the restaurant, and everybody was already eating.

"You could've waited, or at least ordered for me." Karter sat down next to me and took a piece of bacon off my plate.

"Come here, Karter, we not done talking."

"Oop! Looks like Zaddy has spoken, you better go," I whispered in her ear and laughed.

"Shut the hell up, you so extra."

"I see you getting up, though!" She stuck her middle finger up at me and went to sit next to Dez. I turned to Dame, who had just finished eating his food, and licked my lips.

"What you getting into after this, Dame?"

"Shit, my bed, you tryna join me or something?"

"Nah, I like sleeping alone, but we can take care of that in the bathroom."

"You ain't gotta tell me twice."

Dame snatched me out the booth and pulled me to the bathroom in the back of the restaurant. You can call me a hoe if you want, but I don't give a shit. If I want something, I'mma go for it; closed mouths don't get fed. I never did this before, but I was drunk, horny, and single, and Hennything was definitely possible.

I locked the door behind myself and lifted my leather skirt up, exposing my red boy shorts that matched my bra.

Dame picked me up, sat me on the sink, and stood between my legs. I leaned up to kiss his big pink lips and, to my surprise, he kissed me back. I heard the crinkling of the condom opening, so I sat back to get a look at what he was working with. I was in pain just looking at the girth and length of his penis. All the stuff I used to say about light-skinned dudes having small dicks was clearly not true.

"Don't be looking scared now; this what you wanted, right?"

"Yeah, I want it but damn, why you got so much of it?"

"Cause I'm a grown ass man, open up for me."

I spread my legs more, and he eased his member inside of me. I knew my poo nanny would never be the same again, because he was stretching my walls past the limit.

I was biting his shoulder, trying not to scream out, but it wasn't working.

"Fuck Dame, slow down!"

"Mmm, shut up before the whole restaurant hear yo ass, girl."

Dame picked me up off the sink and threw me against the wall, never missing a beat with his strokes.

"You hear that, Mel? She getting wet as hell for me. You loving this shit like I am, ain't you?"

I squeezed my muscles tight, and I felt his body stiffen. He let out an animalistic growl before I heard him snort.

"That was the ugliest sound I ever heard."

"Fuck you." He pulled out of me and placed me on my feet. I had some wipes in my purse, so I gave him one and got a few out to clean myself up.

"Damn, you bit the shit out of me, I see yo little ass teeth marks in my shoulder."

"Oops, yo fault."

"You act like a nigga, that ain't cute."

"I don't care what ain't cute to you."

"I'll break that wall down soon, it's all good."

"Good luck trying."

I walked out of the bathroom with him on my heels.

"Y'all some nasty muhfuckas, I heard you all the way out here."

"Destini, shut up, you ain't heard shit."

"Mel, you ready? I'm tired as hell."

"Yeah, we can go. It's been real, guys, we'll see y'all another day."

Dez and Dame stood up, and Dez wrapped his arm around Karter's shoulder and walked her out to my car.

"I'll be hitting yo line soon, you better answer the phone too."

"I got you, Dez." He kissed her on the forehead and she got in the car, smiling from ear to ear.

"Let me find out you in love already."

"Let me find out you was bussing it open already."

"Touché, nigga. Touché."

"Nasty ass."

"Call it what you want, but I'mma learn you sumn, girl. If Dez is anything like his brother, baaabbbyyyy, you in trouble."

"You might be right. I felt that thang when he was standing behind me, I don't think I'm ready for all that."

"I'm telling you, you not ready. Shit, I wasn't even ready."

"Girl, you are crazy, wake me up when we get home."

Ain't this 'bout a bitch?

She just sat back, got comfortable, and went to sleep. Now, I was forced to stay up alone. I had sobered up a lot since we'd been at the restaurant, and from when I got a dose of Dame. Damn, that nigga was fine. Too bad my ex, Rodney, pretty much fucked it up for the next person.

Have y'all ever gave yo all to a person, only for him to spit in your face? That's exactly what Rodney did to me. About three years ago, I had got pregnant with what would've been our first baby. He told me he didn't think we were ready for a baby because we were still young, blah blah. So, being the dummy I was for him, I got an abortion. Then, a month later, I find out he got somebody else pregnant. She was six fucking months pregnant at that. After being with this man for six years, since I was sixteen fucking years old, he'd been cheating on me all this time and I didn't even know it. I was so heartbroken, I didn't know what to do. Big Mama, who is actually Karter's grandmother, let me move in with them. I was so thankful. I cried like a baby when she died last year. Karter— man, Karter was so hurt. She cried for two months straight. She even quit teaching at the dance studio, and that was her first love. That's why I been fighting so hard for her to get out the house. Tonight, she looked so happy. I know Big Mama was smiling down on us. My best friend was literally my life; if she hurt, I hurt.

Karter

"Karter, if you don't get yo ass up, you gon' be sleeping in the car." I opened my eyes and saw we were parked in front of the house.

"Would you really leave me out here to be bound, gagged, raped, and robbed?"

"You dramatic as hell; you would probably get robbed at the most, maybe hit by a stray bullet."

"That's terrible, Mel."

"Nah boo, that's life when you live in Chicago, you know that."

We got in the house, and Melodee went to her room, then I went to mine after I grabbed some water to take this aspirin. I stripped out of my clothes and took another shower; since my hair was smelling like cigarettes, I had to wash it, and that's the main reason why I didn't go to the clubs.

I laid down and finished reading. I swear, this Kindle was my life, especially when I was home alone. Talk about peace.

I woke up the next morning feeling like shit. I knew I was going to be throwing up all day, because my stomach was tore up from mixing light and dark liquor last night. I don't know why I did that mess, but I was definitely paying for it now.

"Karter, you throw up loud as hell. I heard you all the way in my room."

"Bitch, bring me a Gatorade, you should've came to check on me instead of talking shit."

She walked into the room with a blunt and some Gatorade. "This all you need, and I guarantee you gon' feel 100% better."

She handed it to me to light, and I inhaled slowly. I tried not to smoke so much since I was a dancer; I couldn't be all winded.

"You keep that, I'll be back with some food. I wanted some Chili's, so I ordered to-go."

"Ok."

She left and I laid back in the bed, smoking my blunt. I was glad I didn't have any classes today; I would've had to cancel.

I stayed in bed all day and thankfully, Mel took care of me.

The next day, I was up early to make it to practice on time.

I was the only dance instructor left, and it sucked because everyone else went to different companies.

I was able to partner with a local instructor who taught ballet, and she agreed to come in and teach us some techniques. When I took over, I was planning on getting us into more competitions, and hopefully, finding myself an assistant to help full-time too. But right now, my focus was on getting enough money to buy the studio. I could've used the money that I got from Big Mama's insurance policy, but then that would have left me with absolutely nothing.

After practice, I was able to get a ride with one of the parents, and I didn't have to take the bus, thankfully. When I walked into the house, Dame and Melodee were sitting on the couch watching a movie.

"Hey, y'all."

"Wassup, Karter."

"Hey boo, how was practice?"

"It was cool; we had a ballet instructor come in to show us some steps that I'm going to add into a stand."

"That's wassup."

"Yeah, but I'm going to shower and go to bed. Nice seeing you again, Dame." I walked to my room and flopped on my bed. I checked my phone for the hundredth time, and I still didn't have any texts from Dez. I was mad I didn't get his number, but I guess that's over and done with now.

****

It had been about two weeks since I met Dez, and he still hadn't called me. I was feeling a little salty, like damn, did he only talk to me so his brother could talk to Mel? I had been seeing and hearing Dame creeping in and out of the house, so I knew they were still in touch.

I had just left from the dance studio and was walking to the bus stop when my phone vibrated in my pocket.

Wya?

About to get on the bus, why?

You cooking tonight?

Hell no, Mel, it's 8 o'clock!

Huuuh fine… well, hurry up then, I'm ordering pizza.

Beep!

Beep!

I turned around and saw a matte black Jeep with dark ass tints riding slowly next to me.

The dance studio I worked at was near 95th and King Drive, and it wasn't the best place to be walking late at night.

I started speed-walking and heard a door open and close behind me. I start panicking and looking for anywhere I could run and get help. I was literally the only person on this side of the street, and the bus was nowhere to be seen. If I got snatched right now, all these mothafuckas was gon' do was record the shit and put it on social media.

"Karter! Slow yo scary ass down."

I turned around and saw Dez jogging up to me, laughing and looking sexy as hell. He was dressed in an all-black suit, looking real Zaddy-ish, as Melodee was say. I breathed a sigh of relief as he approached me.

He grabbed my big Nike gym bag off my shoulder and wrapped his arm around my shoulder.

"Girl, you sweaty as hell, what the hell you been doing?" He helped me into the truck and tossed my bag in the backseat.

"Shut up, I just got out of practice, for yo information."

"What, football practice, cuz you a little tart, baby girl."

"No, asshole. I dance, so you stop with your jokes."

"What kind of dancing you be doing, you be twerking and shit?"

"I'm done talking to you, you play too much."

"Aite, aite I'm done. What kind of dancing you do, for real?"

"Well, I teach majorette for ages 5 to 17, or until they graduate high school, but I also dance contemporary and hip-hop."

"So, you probably flexible as hell, right?" He had a sneaky grin on his face, and he was making his eyebrows jump. I had to turn to look out the window to stop myself from smiling.

"You're so inappropriate."

"Shit, I was just asking; it don't hurt to ask questions, right?"

"Yeah right, it don't hurt to ask questions, but you'll get hurt for asking the wrong questions."

"Ok, with yo tough ass. Where you stay at, and why you out walking this late?"

"I stay on 108th and Throop. And I don't have a car, obviously, or I would be driving. That's just not a top priority for me right now."

"So, what's top priority for you?"

"I'm saving to buy the dance studio I teach at. The owner is moving soon, and I just don't want the doors to close permanently."

"Aw, well shit, there you go. At least you doing what you gotta do and not spending money on bundles and makeup. All the shit I got ain't fall in my lap, I made shit happen, so I ain't knocking yo hustle."

I pointed out my house, and Dez pulled up in the front. He put his truck in park and got out to help me, then he grabbed my bag and walked me to the front door.

"Thank you for the ride."

"Anytime, baby girl. Here, just call me on this, and it bet not be no other nigga's numbers in there either."

He handed me a red iPhone 7 Plus that was still in the box, and I had to look at him like he lost his mind.

"You know I got a phone already, right?"

"Yeah, that weak ass Samsung, you can't even Facetime."

"Whatever, I like my android, ain't nothing special about these phones."

I reached out for my bag, and he bent down and smashed his lips into mine. I was feeling bold, so I slipped my tongue in his mouth.

"Mmmm, get yo hot ass in the house before you get yourself in trouble out here, Karter."

The front door opened, and Melodee was standing there smirking with her arms folded across her chest.

"Well, hello to you, Dez. Karter, nice to see you made it home safely."

"Wassup? I'll hit you up later, Karter. I gotta get down to the club." He walked to his running truck and pulled off.

"Here I was, worried about you and you on the porch about to get dicked down."

"Don't be dramatic, Mel."

"I'm not, I was about to get some popcorn and enjoy the show."

"Like the show you and Dame been putting on the last few weeks?"

"Now, you the one being dramatic."

Our rooms were literally on the opposite side of the house, but those two were always loud as hell. I gave her the 'now you know' look, and she just rolled her eyes at me.

"Whatever, I ordered from Waldo Cooney's, so it should be here in a minute. Bitch, when you get a new phone?"

"He just gave this to me."

"Let me find out!"

I laughed and walked off to my room so I could shower and relax in my bed. I played with this new phone before I ended up dozing off with it still in my hand.

The loud ring from the cellphone in my hand woke me up out of my deep slumber, and I hurriedly answered it so I could stop the noise.

"Hello?"

"Damn, it took you long enough, answer yo Facetime." I sat up looked at the phone. "You look sexy as hell when you first wake up, even with that lil' slob on yo cheek and yo hair all over yo head."

I started wiping at my face, and I heard him and Dame laughing at me.

"Shut up, it's three in the morning, Dez."

"Shit, I know. I'm about to head up outta the club in a minute."

"Ay, ask her where Melodee at."

"Man, I ain't asking her shit, you better call her phone."

Dez and Dame were going back and forth with each other, and I just got out the bed to see if Melodee had the decency to save me some food.

"What you doing?"

"About to warm my food up. I been sleep since I got home."

"Aw ok, you feel like some company?"

"Now?"

"Yeah now, I'll be there in twenty minutes. You bet not go back to sleep or I'mma be climbing through yo window."

"I'll be up, come on."

I set the phone down on the island and ate my pizza and cheese fries. When I was done, I ran to my room to brush my teeth and put on some cuter pajamas.

Come to the door

I put my hair in a messy bun on top of my head and went to the front door.

When I opened the door, Dez and Dame were standing on the porch waiting, and both of them looked either drunk or high, maybe both.

"Sup, sis?"

"Um hey, I think Mel still sleep."

"I know, I'm 'bout to wake her up." He started humping the air, and I was dying laughing at him.

"He drunk, come on, where yo room? I'm tired as fuck, been up almost 36 hours straight."

"Why?" I led him to the back of the house where my room was, and I closed the door.

He started getting undressed and slid into my bed only wearing his boxer briefs and a tank.

"I'm mad you got this little ass bed."

"It's a queen size, and it's plenty room for me."

"Not for me, though, look at my feet damn near hanging on the floor."

"Well, buy me a bigger bed then."

"Aite, I'll do it tomorrow."

"I was just playing, Dez, don't bring no damn bed in here."

"Aite, well don't say shit you don't mean. What time you gotta be up in the morning?"

"Saturdays are my early days, gotta be out by 9 o'clock."

"Aw naw, fuck that shit, you can take my Jeep. I'll get a ride home from bro."

He pulled me close so I was laying on his chest, and I just stared up at his side profile.

"Stop being a creep and go to sleep, Karter."

"How you know what I'm doing with your eyes closed?"

"I feel yo big ass eyes piercing through my soul."

"Whatever."

"Goodnight, Karter."

Dame

"Dame? Dame, what the hell, get up!"

I opened one of my eyes and saw Melodee standing over me like she had an attitude.

"What you want, girl, Shit, I'm tryna sleep."

"Well go home, how the hell you get in here anyway?"

"The door, nigga, how else? What time is it?"

"It's time for you to get your ass up and go home."

"Fuck it, since yo bald head ass wanna play and wake me up and shit."

"Nigga, you was naked?!"

"Hell yeah, I was gon' wake you up with this dick, but I was too fucked up."

I threw my clothes on and walked out her room with her mugging me the whole time. Dez was sitting on the couch in their living going through his phone, and when he saw me, he stood up and straightened his clothes up.

"Bro, I need you to take me to the crib."

"Where yo whip?" I locked their bottom lock and walked to my car.

"I let Karter take it, I ain't feel like getting up when she did."

"Booaa, if you don't get yo crazy in love ass outta here. You don't even let me drive me drive them bitches."

"Cuz, yo ass can't drive, nigga."

"But you hopped yo ass in the car with my non-driving ass, though."

"Shut up and drive."

I sped and dropped him off at home, and went down the street to my house. We both stayed in Oak Lawn, and it was a good twenty to twenty-five-minute drive from the girls' crib.

When I got in the house, I showered, laid down across my sectional, and turned SportsCenter on.

Melodee had me fucked up, though, tryna act like she ain't want me in her bed and shit. Like I was just a booty call or something. She always had my ass calling her first and shit, unless she wanted to fuck. She swore she was a nigga, and I wasn't feeling that shit at all. But, I guess I had to show her how the game was really played if she wanna go there. I'd have her ass replaced in the quickness, but I didn't want no thirsty ass chick.

Just when I was dozing off, I heard my phone ringing and it was Dez calling.

"Talk to me."

I need you to handle the club tonight. I'm tryna do some shit with Karter, I might take her out."

"Damn bro, you pulling all the tricks out, ain't you? I got you, though, ain't like I got shit else to do. You need to tell Karter to talk to her buddy so she can get off that bullshit. Nigga, I'm tryna ride off in the sunset with y'all ass."

"Man, you a grown ass man, I ain't telling her nothing. You can't handle little Mel, bro?"

"Uglass boy, don't play with me. But I'm in charge of yo bachelor party, though, congratulations man."

"Fuck outta here."

Click

This nigga hung up on me. Dez could play all he wanted to, but I knew he was really feeling shorty. I couldn't remember the last time he actually put time into a female. Nigga was always tight as hell about everything; now he was acting like a somewhat normal muhfucka.

***

I was at the club, and it was lit as fuck tonight. Saturdays were always the most live for us. Instead of being cooped in the office like Dez' ass, I was down on the main floor, mingling with the patrons.

I was at the bar talking to Mimi, who was helping bartend, when I saw Melodee storming over to me.

"So, we ignoring each other now?"

"I been busy."

One of her eyebrows raised, and she nodded her head up and down.

"Aw ok." She was about to walk off until Mimi opened her big ass mouth.

"Who is that, Dame?"

"Don't fucking worry about who I am, home girl, and direct any questions you have about me to me."

"Awwww, this must be the chick you fucked in the bathroom."

Me and Melodee both looked at her crazy. I didn't know who told her that shit, but I hated for people to tell shit that wasn't meant to be shared.

The way Melodee was grilling me, it was like I was the one who told her that shit, but I didn't brag on my dick.

"That's how you doing it, Dame?"

"Ay, don't even try to play me like a—"

"Goofy? Because that's exactly what you are, but you good, bro." She cut me off and directed her attention back to Mimi.

"And bitch, I hope you don't think you doing something, cuz ain't no shame in what I did. Ask Dame how tight it was, though."

She switched away through the crowd and toward the door, and I swear my dick jumped a little bit.

Mimi was just standing there looking stupid with her mouth open.

"Who told you that shit?"

"A little birdie."

"Yeah? Well, the next time you open yo mouth about some shit you heard from a damn bird, you gon' be unemployed."

I walked off, pissed as hell. This was not how I wanted this shit with me and Melodee to go. Besides the fact that she stubborn as hell, she was actually a dope ass female and besides the sex, we had fun together. I think I was gon' fire Mimi's ass anyway. Dumb bitch.

Karter

I didn't get home from rehearsal until after 5 o'clock, and I was so tired. Dez had texted me earlier and told me to be dressed to go out, and I didn't know what he had planned. I asked him how I should dress, and he said he didn't care. Like, what the fuck? He told me to be ready at eight, so I had a little time before I had to get ready. Right now, I was laid across my bed, catching up on my reading on my Kindle.

I had just finished *She's Different From the Other Ones* by Dee Ann, and just started reading *Us Before Anything* by Ms. Brii. Between those two, they were going to make me have a heart attack. I was in love with two people who don't even exist. Between Roman and Lah? Lawd, help me!

"Oh my God, bestie, my blood is boiling." Melodee had burst into my room and snatched my Kindle out my hand.

"What the hell is wrong with you, Mel?"

"I went to the fucking club, because Dame was ignoring me, right? I'm seeing this nigga read my text message, and he wasn't replying. ALL FUCKING NIGHT."

"How you know he read your message?"

"Girl, I forgot you're new to the iPhone family. But, you gotta wait until after I finish telling you this fuck shit. Soooo, I popped and went to his office. I didn't see him in there, so I checked the cameras and saw him sitting at the bar skinning and grinning and shit, so I go down there. I ask this man why he ain't text me back, and do you know what he said?"

I sat waiting for her to tell me what he said, but she was staring at me like she was waiting for me to say something.

"He gon' say *I was busy*. I was thinking, aw ok bitch, you about to be busy taking my foot out yo ass. But I ain't want him to send my head through a wall or something. So, I just said aw ok, and I was gon' leave. I WAS GOING TO LEAVE. But, the bitch behind the bar opened her big ass mouth. Gon' ask am I the girl he fucked in the bathroom. Biiiihhhh, I wanted grab her by that wopsided ass wig and clean the floor with her. But I didn't, I walked away, but I wish I didn't walk away. I don't think I'm gon' be able to sleep tonight because I'mma be thinking about this shit. Like, why didn't you beat her ass, Mel? Bestie, you know I must be growing. I wouldn't have even thought about it. God is working on me, whew, woosah."

I was trying so hard not to laugh, but I couldn't help myself.

"Don't laugh at me, Karter, I was three seconds from popping that hoe in her mouth. Somebody need to tell that hoe she'd rather tongue kiss an alligator than fuck with me."

"You're a psycho baby, Mel, we gon' get you help one day. But can you help me put together a cute outfit?"

"Where you going?"

"I don't know, Dez texted me and said he was taking me out."

"At least one of us is having some luck."

"I think you're overreacting, on Dame's behalf. I can't see him going around telling people his business.

And, if it's the same girl I almost slapped when I was there, we can go back and tag team her."

"See, this is why I need you in my life; you get me, baby. But I ain't fucking with Dame, that shit just turned me all the way off. Ain't nothing worse than a nigga that run his mouth like a bitch."

"You so damn stubborn, everybody ain't Rodney. I'm telling you, just talk to him, don't miss yo beat."

"Girl, I ain't missing shit, trust me. Anyway, let's see what you got in this closet."

We went through my closet and picked out some black wash jeans, and a pink off the shoulder, ruffled bodysuit. I had a pair of pink flatform sandals I never got to wear from Charlotte Russe, so I was going to put them on.

"What you doing to your hair?"

"I'm fixing my damn bun, I'm not going through all them extra steps tonight."

"Are you gon' at least wear a little makeup?"

"That's a no for me."

"Ugh, fine."

Melodee walked out, and I laid back down to finish my reading.

Dez was literally texting me at 7:59, telling me to open the door.

"You're very punctual, I like that."

"Shit, I can say the same about you. Usually, women be slow as hell."

"You always go straight for the insults, I see."

"My bad, let me start over. You look beautiful as hell, Karter, is that ok with you?"

"Thank you. I see you took a break from the business look, I like it."

Dez was wearing a white Chicago White Sox jersey, khaki cargo shorts, and some fresh white Air Force Ones.

We walked outside, and there was an all-black Porsche Cayenne parked in front. When he opened the door, I admired the cream-colored leather interior; it even had that new car smell I loved. I think I liked this truck more than his Jeep.

"This is nice, you just got this?"

"Naw, I had it for a few months. I don't really drive it like it that, though."

"So, where we going?"

"Lazer X."

"All the way in Addison? That's like an hour drive, Dez. I'm glad I got some flats in my purse, you should've let me know that bit of information.

"This just give us time to talk, you can start."

"You know about me, though."

"Not really. Where's yo family?"

"All I have is Melodee now, my grandmother passed last year. She had Alzheimer's and after a while, she just let go."

"Sorry for your loss."

"Thanks, what about you?"

"My OG still alive and kicking. Ain't really mess with my pops like that, so ain't nothing to tell. When he died, I took over. You already know Dame and Destini, so that's everybody."

"So, what did you do before you opened the club?"

When I asked the question I had been dying to ask, his entire posture changed, and he cleared his throat.

"I did some shit I'm not proud of, but it was for my family, and I'd do it again if I had to."

"I wouldn't judge you off your past; like you said, you did it for your family."

We were riding and talking about everything, from our favorite food to our favorite TV show. He told me *Hey Arnold* was his favorite show to watch growing up, and I laughed so hard. Before I knew it, he was parking and helping me out of the truck.

He set us up for the three-game special, and I was hyped to get started. We were literally the only people in the building besides the worker in the front.

"Where is everybody? I always hear that it be packed in here."

"I had them close it down. I wasn't about to be playing with other niggas, fuck around and have to shoot somebody for real."

"Well, I sure hope your gun isn't on you right now, I'm not trying to die tonight."

"Aw naw, baby, it's always on me, but I ain't gone do that to you."

"Ok, I'll never know with you."

"Give me a kiss for good luck."

"Nope; if you win, you can have it, though." I walked off quickly into the maze when the lights went out, and I heard Dez laughing behind me.

Dezmund "Dez"

We were on our third game, and so far, it was tied. We made a bet that the loser had to do whatever the winner said. She won the first game and was being too cocky, so I had to show her who I was.

Right now, I ain't know where her little ass was at.

EEEOOOEEEOOO

Game Over!

"Yesss! You walked right past me!"

Karter was behind me, dancing and jumping up and down. The lights came back on, and we walked back up to the front desk and took off the equipment.

"That was so much fun, I'm hungry now, tho."

"Aite, you wanna get something out here or when we get back to the city?"

"What's there to eat out here?"

"I don't know, Bugs, we can look when we get in the car."

"Bugs?"

"Yeah, you got them two big teeth like a bunny, so who's the most popular bunny besides the Easter bunny?"

"My big mama spent a lot of money getting my teeth fixed, I can't help how they are."

"You good, I like that shit."

We got in my ride, and I turned the air on. She pulled her phone out and started looking up restaurants.

"Only thing that's really open is a Mexican spot."

"That's cool with me. Put it in the GPS."

We arrived at La Hacienda and walked in, hand in hand. She had her fingers interlocked in mine, and I was lowkey smiling hard as hell. I couldn't explain the feeling I got when I was around Karter, but I knew I wanted it all the time. Only thing is, I ain't never did this shit before, and it take a lot for me to trust somebody, so this was going to be a challenge for me. Those first two weeks after I met her, I had somebody watching her every move. I had to know if she was shady before I even pursued her further.

"All of this look so good, but I know what I want."

The server approached us and asked if we were ready to order.

"Yeah, you go ahead and order first."

"I want a torta, but I want the guacamole on the side, and I want some of those chips and salsa."

"Is that it?"

"Shit, I hope so."

"Shut up, Dez, that's it. Well, I want a mango Margarita, on ice, with sugar around the rim too, the biggest one you got."

"And for you, sir?"

"I want a combination fajita, no onions and add sour cream."

"And to drink?"

"I want a bottle of water."

"Ok, I'll put this in and I'll be right back."

"What you drinking for?"

"Who comes to a Mexican restaurant and doesn't drink? Well, besides you?"

"I guess. It's your world, Karter."

"Thank you."

Her drink was brought out with my bottle of water, and she was just staring at it, amazed. My phone buzzed on the table, so I picked it up and Karter's attention came straight to me. It was only Dame, so I turned my phone around to show her. I ain't have shit to hide anyway.

"You didn't have to do that."

"Naw, I know how women think when phones get to going off after ten o'clock."

Bro, Mimi ass gotta go!

What happened now?

I responded to Dame and set my phone back down. Ever since Mimi had that run-in with Karter, I was thinking about firing her ass too.

Man, I'll tell you tomorrow, I'm ready to get the hell outta here

Well, don't fire Mimi until the club close nigga, lol

Lol, you ain't shit boa

I put my phone up, and Karter was halfway done with her margarita.

"Damn girl, slow down."

"It's so good, I think I want a strawberry one next."

"Yo ass an alcoholic, ma?"

"No, believe it or not, I'm not really a drinker."

"Ahhh shit."

"But I'm not a crazy drunk!" She was laughing, and it seemed as if her eyes were sparkling too.

Our food was brought out, and she really ordered another drink. She was eating her food, and you would've swore somebody was starving her.

"Don't stare at me."

"You good, baby girl. So, what is it that I gotta do for you since I lost?"

"You gotta come to the recital; my baby class is performing, and I am too."

"So, I get a chance to see you dance?"

"Yeah."

"I got you. I'll be there right in the front. Can I invite some people?"

"Yeah, that's fine."

By the time we finished eating, it was a quarter to midnight and the restaurant was getting ready to close. I paid the tab and left a tip on the table before we left out. I could tell Karter was faded, but she was trying to play it off.

"Do you want to go home, or you riding with me?"

"I'm riding with you."

The ride from Addison to my house in Oak Lawn was only thirty minutes, but Karter was sleep already. There was a gate around my property, and if you didn't have the code, you couldn't get in.

The gate opened and closed right behind me, and I pulled right up to the front door. When the truck cut off, Karter sat up and was looking around.

"Damn, this house is nice as hell."

"Thank you."

"I didn't even know houses like this were out here."

"It wasn't, until I had it built."

"Man, must be nice. Big Mama owned the house we're staying in, and when she started getting real bad, she switched everything to me. I'm never moving outta that house."

"What if you get a family or something?"

"Then, me and family are going to be living in that house."

"Yo husband wouldn't have any say so in that?"

"I mean, if he loves me, he'll understand and wouldn't try to make me move."

"That's a funny way of thinking about it."

"Yeah, well it's my way of thinking. Anyway, I love these marble floors, I bet your feet be cold when you're walking barefoot."

"I have flip flops on if I'm walking around."

"I'll never wear shoes, matter fact. Oh my goodness, this is life."

She took her shoes off and was just walking through the house on her tippy toes. We got to my bedroom and went right to my bed and sat down.

"This bed is huge, what size is this?"

"Californian King, I need room to stretch. I'm 6'5, I need that."

"Damn, I knew you were tall, but I ain't know you was that tall. I'm only 5'5", you're a whole foot taller than me."

"That cool, so when is your recital?"

"Three weeks from today. I'm probably going to be busy because I'mma be practicing 24/7 like the week before. That's on top of practice with my baby class. I can't wait to see them in their little tutus."

"You wearing a tutu?"

"No, I'm not wearing a tutu, you damn pervert. I'm dancing in a contemporary group, then I have a solo to end the show."

"Damn, ok. I can't wait to see it. I'll provide front door service so we can ride together."

"Ok, I'll like that."

I gave her a shirt to sleep in, and she snuggled right under me. The smell of raspberries was in her hair and the shit smelled good as hell. I could definitely get used to this.

***

It was the day of Karter's recital, and I closed the club just for today. I didn't care about the money I was losing by doing this. I was going to make sure she had all the support she could.

Dame, Destini, and Melodee were already on their way and surprising her there. I just hoped Dame and Melodee didn't act a fool in there. I even had my moms coming; she didn't know where she was going, and I told Dame and Destini not to tell her until I got there with Karter.

"I'm so nervous, my hands are sweating like crazy. I swear, I'm going to throw up."

"Bugs, you gotta relax. That's just pre- show jitters or whatever that shit is called. You know you gon' kill it, bae."

"Thank you for coming, Dez. I really appreciate this."

"Anytime, I'll always be your number one fan. I'll even spend the rest of the day rubbing your body down."

"That sounds so good, but you need to feed me first. I want a big ass burger from somewhere."

"I got you. When we leave outta here, I'll get you taken care of."

I parked and carried Karter's gym bag inside the building. Her little hand was really sweating, and I had to stop and give her a pep talk.

"Karter, come on, ma. I hear yo heart beating out of your chest. You need to breathe before yo ass pass out up in here. I know this ain't your first performance."

"It's my first performance since Big Mama died. She used to come see every performance, even when she got real sick. This was the one thing she always remembered."

A few tears fell from her eyes, and I wiped them with my thumb and gave her a kiss on the lips.

"Look, Big Mama is proud of you, and I'm proud of you. How you gon' be out here all nervous and you got these kids looking at you?"

"You right, I need to get my life together."

"Kaayyyyy!" Mel came from behind her, and they hugged tight. Karter greeted Dame, Destini, and my mom, and my mom pulled her into a hug.

"Thank y'all so much for coming, I really appreciate this."

"No probably, honey. I see them people waving you down, so you gone head, but me and you are going to have our own little talk."

"Yes, ma'am. I'll see you later, Dez."

She walked away and into the double doors that all the other dancers were going in.

Karter

I had just performed my solo, and everyone was clapping loudly and cheering. The curtains closed, and I broke down and said a prayer.

"You did great, Karter! I swear, I shed a tear."

People were hugging me, and I couldn't take my smile off my face. When I got changed out of my costume, Dez was standing with a big bouquet of sunflowers. I told him those were my favorite, and I was surprised he actually remembered.

"Man bae, I don't know what you call that, but it was sexy as hell."

"Thank you, crazy."

Melodee walked up to me and had a tear-stained face. She hugged me and, I held onto her extra tight. She knew my struggle to get back into dancing, and this was a huge accomplishment for me.

"I'm so proud of you, bestie, you did great."

"That was so good. I recorded it on my camera, if you want a copy." Dez's mom was being extra nice and gave me another hug. This was our first time meeting, and I was actually kind of mad he didn't warn me ahead of time, but I was glad she was nice. I witnessed some crazy stuff with girls and their boyfriend's mothers.

"Thank you so much."

"No problem, honey. I'm ready to go lay down, so we can't really talk. Dez, bring her by tomorrow for Sunday dinner. I got a good feeling about her."

"Aite, Ma."

"Karter, you killed that shit."

"Thank you, Destini, and what made you dye your hair blonde?"

"Because I look good, and I can do that."

"Girl, bye."

Everyone walked out the building and went their separate ways to their vehicles.

"I can't believe you didn't tell me that your mom was coming, that's just wrong."

"How? Moms cool as hell."

"It still would've been nice to know ahead of time."

"My bad, I won't do it again."

"I can't wait until these dry out. I'm gon' tear these seeds up."

"You act like a fat lady, Karter, for real."

"I don't care, would you still talk to me if I was fat?"

"Yeah, I'd grab on your love handles." Dez rubbed on my thigh, and I had to cross my legs. We have yet to do anything physical, and I didn't think I could wait any longer.

We ended up at Black Oak to eat, and I couldn't wait to get my food. I ordered a Farm House burger, and my stomach was thanking me.

I ate my whole burger and had some of Dez's nachos. By the time we were leaving, it felt like I had gained 20 pounds.

"I need a nap so bad, I feel like pig."

"Yo hungry ass just killed an eight-ounce burger. I bet you is tired."

"You can sleep when you get in the house. I got a question, though?"

"What?"

"I know you got mad when I replaced yo bed, but I got you sumn and you might be mad, orrrr, you might be happy; it depends, I guess."

We pulled up to his house, and there was a brand-new BMW parked inside the gate with a red bow on it. My mouth was hanging open.

"Is that mine?"

"Yeah, that yours." He parked and came around to the passenger side to open my door.

"Come on and get out. I know you tired of driving my truck, so I got you something smaller. It's in yo name and it's paid off, so don't worry about nothing."

"This is nice, I'm in love, look at it."

"You in love with me or the car?"

"The car, crazy."

"Well, I'm in love with you."

"Huh?"

"You heard me."

"You don't love me, hush Dezmund."

"Get out the car and come on."

I followed him into house, and he picked me up. I wrapped my legs around his waist, and my arms around his neck. We were kissing, and he was walking to the bedroom without even looking. He laid me on the bed and pulled my tank over my head. He was caressing my nipples, and I was enjoying the feel of his hands on my body.

"Yo moans sexy as fuck, bae."

I couldn't say anything because while he was talking, he slipped his finger in my tunnel and was snaking it around, sending shocks through my body.

"Dezzzz."

"What, baby? You gon' give me that shit?'

"Yeessssss."

He snatched my shorts off and attacked my southern lips with his mouth. The second his tongue touched me, I was cumming and trying to scoot away from him.

"Sit the fuck still, Karter."

My mouth was hanging open in an O, and I swear I was seeing white doves flying over my head.

"You taste good as hell, turn over."

I got on all fours and felt Dez's monster poking at my opening.

"Ahhhh."

"Fuck."

He entered me, and instant regret filled my head. I saw what Melodee was trying to warn me about.

He started going slow, then started pounding into me when I started throwing it back to match his strokes. I was feeling my third orgasm creeping up, and he didn't seem to be stopping anytime soon.

"Turn over."

I followed his lead completely and was on my back with my legs on his shoulder.

My moans turned into screams, and I was scratching his back up.

I now knew what Trey Songz meant by *'Imma take yo pain if you take mine.'*

"Fuuuccckkk. Come ride yo dick, bae."

I got on top and lowered myself down onto him. I was moving my body to the song playing in my head while Dez had a death grip on my hips.

"I'm finna come, bae, but I don't wanna pull out."

He sped up his rhythm, and I felt like I was on a mechanical bull.

Dez's body got stiff, and he started moving me up and down slowly. His eyebrows were scrunched up, and he was staring at me like he was mad.

I laid down on his chest with him still inside of me, and we were both breathing hard.

"Come on, let's go shower so you can take yo nap."

"I can't move, I'm so tired."

My eyes were still closed, and Dez stood up and carried me to the bathroom. He had a shower bench, so he sat me on it while he got the water right. When it was nice and warm, he took a loofah and squeezed some of my Bed, Bath and Beyond body wash on it.

Dez took his time washing every inch of my body, while I just sat there loving it all.

I stood up to rinse my body off while Dez washed himself up. I stepped out the shower and grabbed my big, fluffy white robe to put on. When I walked into the room, I dried my body off and rubbed my Aveeno Ultra Hydrating Moisturizer all over.

Dez came out of the bathroom, and I was already halfway asleep. I heard him smack his lips, but I was too tired to say anything. Before long, sleep took over my body and I welcomed it with open arms.

***

The next morning when I woke up, Dez had me in a bear hug and I couldn't move. I really had to use the bathroom, so I tried to slide down out of his hold, but when I moved, he grabbed me tighter.

"Dezmund!"

"Hmmm?"

"Let me go, I gotta pee."

"My bad, baby."

I got out the bed, and it felt like I was hit by an 18-wheeler, twice! I cursed all the way to the bathroom, where I did my regular morning routine. When my teeth were brushed, I went back into the room and saw Dez wasn't in the bed any more. I checked my phone and saw I had some messages from Melodee.

I need a new job ASAP

Why

Tired of being in the damn house! I'm considering selling drugs, or ass sumn exciting hell!!

"What you laughing at?"

"Mel, she complaining about her job." Mel worked at home as a supervisor for a virtual call center, so she was literally always home.

"Tell her come interview to be my club manager."

"Are you serious?"

"Hell yeah. Since we fired Mimi, me and Dame had to pick up her shit too. We ain't really think that through."

"That bitch needed to go. Now that she don't work there, I can pull her on her ass."

"You wildin'"

"Naw, I'm serious, but I'll let her know."

"Tell her come to Moms' crib, we gon' be there all day. Sundays, she cooks breakfast and dinner, so we all just chill at her house."

"Who is we? Like, who's going to be there?"

"Shit Dame, Destini, and me."

"What am I supposed to wear? I packed some sundresses and shorts, but I think they'll expose too much skin."

"Why you tripping? Mama already seen you half naked last night on the stage. You good, bae."

He kissed my forehead and walked into his closet.

"That's not helping!"

I sat on the bed and texted Melodee, asking if she wanted to come with us today, and about the job at the club. Surprisingly, she said yeah to both; she had been ignoring Dame so long, I didn't think she would ever be in his presence willingly again. That only meant Melodee was about to be on her get back.

Melodee

When Karter texted me about that job, I was gon' say heeeelllll naw, but then I thought *forget that, I'm about to make my coins.* I'm sure they paid more than what I was making now, and I'd get to be at the club turnt— perfect job.

The only big con was Damien Wright. Last night, I did a good job of ignoring him, but I don't know how much longer I could do it. His beard had grown a lot, and lawd knows how I love me a man with a beard. I just wish it was on somebody else.

Karter texted me an address in South Holland, so I got up to get ready so I wouldn't be late leaving out. My twist out was already on point, so I just had to throw on my clothes. I was going to throw on something to fuck Dame's head up, but I talked myself outta it. Instead, I threw on white crop top with my overall shorts, and my sneakers from Aldo.

I locked up the house and walked to my car. I saw Rodney's car roll past, then he reversed down the street and came back. I rolled my eyes as he blocked my car and got out.

"Where you on yo way to?"

"Um, excuse you, do I look like one of yo baby mamas to you? Don't question me, Rodney, now can you move yo car so I can leave?"

"Why you acting like you don't miss me?"

"Newsflash, it's not an act. I really don't miss yo ass."

"Aite, keep playing, ain't nobody else gon' put up with that attitude you got, Melodee, remember that."

"Yeah, thanks for the words of encouragement." I got in my car and waited for him to pull off again.

I put the address Karter sent me into my GPS and tried to find the perfect song to ride to. I was that person who couldn't pull off until I found the best song to play that matched my mood. I found "Unforgettable" by French Montana and pulled off from the house, nodding my head. Since we stayed directly by the expressway exit, I hopped on I-57 North so I could merge onto Highway 94 and head to the suburbs.

Their mother's house was a big, pretty, brown brick house, and the driveway was huge. I couldn't wait to see what the inside looked like. I texted Karter when I was outside, and I saw Dame's car pull up at the same time.

"Deep breaths, Mel. You're not mad anymore. Remember, you need a job." I was talking aloud to myself because I swear when I saw his face, I got mad all over again.

He got out his car and walked up to me.

"What you doing here, Melly Mel?"

"I was invited."

"Aw ok, that's wassup, thought you was stalking me or something."

"Nigga please, you ain't nothing to stalk."

"Damn Melodee, you don't see me over here?"

"My bad, Destini, you know I couldn't miss you with that bright ass blonde hair."

"You a hater, bro, all y'all some haters. Y'all know I look good."

We were all laughing and walking to the house. The front door was open, and Karter came out looking confused, but cute as hell. She was wearing a nude sundress and had her hair down and flowing in the wind, giving me straight life.

"What y'all laughing at?"

"Nothing, nosey. You look cute, and you glowing. You finally got some, didn't you?"

"Will you shut up? I'll tell you later, you talking all loud like his mama ain't in there."

"Yo scary ass."

We walked into the house, and there was a sunken dining room on the right, and a big movie theater type living room on the left.

Their mother, or Ma as she told me to call her, came into view from the kitchen, and she walked to me first and gave me a hug.

"Hey, Ma."

"Hey, gorgeous. You slaying, honey."

"Ma, who taught you that word?" I laughed with everyone else.

"I ain't use it right or something?"

"Naw you good, she just hating Ma." Dame hugged her next, and I just rolled my eyes at him.

"Wassup, Mel? Step into my temporary office right quick." Dez appeared from the back of the house, and I followed him back there.

"How are you doing today, Dez?"

"You ain't gotta be fake professional with me. The job is yours if you're going to take it serious. I'm a pretty cool person, but when it come to my money, I'm a different type of beast."

"As you should be. I can guarantee, I take my money just as serious as the next person. When do you want me to start?"

"Tomorrow. I'll have yo keys and alarm code by the time we leave today."

"I have a tiny request, though."

"And what's that?"

"I want the office that's all the way in the back."

"Yo lil' ass really was snooping through that bitch, huh?"

"I didn't take nothing, though, I'm just nosey."

"Aite, you got it, and I don't want no personal bullshit going on in the club. It is a business at the end of the day."

"I don't have any personal bullshit, so we're good."

Soon as the words left my mouth, here come Dame poking his head in the office.

"Ma said come eat."

"Aite, and Melodee is our new manager, so I'll start showing her the ropes tomorrow morning."

"Sounds good to me. Welcome to the family, Mel." Dame smirked at me and left back out the door.

We made it to the table, and it was set up like the Last Supper or something, and this was only breakfast. She had pancakes, Belgian waffles, French toast, and regular toast directly in the middle, then the rest of the food was surrounding it.

"Were some other people coming?" I leaned over and whispered to Destini.

I was sitting between Dame and Destini, and he kept trying to touch my hand. He was smelling good and I was tempted to hug him so I could smell my clothes later. Don't judge me.

"Naw, Ma always cook like this. I think that's why them niggas so tall. I can't eat as much as them."

I looked to my right and saw Dame's plate was full of literally some of everything that was on the table. When I looked up at Dez, his plate looked the same, but he had fruit on the side. Karter was making the same 'Wtf' face I was. Their mom noticed our faces and she laughed at us.

"I guess y'all never saw my boys eat like that before."

"These ain't no damn boys eating like that, excuse my language Ma, but this can't be healthy. I know y'all plumbing be messed up."

"Mel!"

"Karter! What?"

Karter put her head down, and Dame started laughing with a mouth full of food.

"You need to close your mouth and finish chewing your food, because if you get some slop in my lap, we going to have some problems, Damien."

I turned back to eating my food, and all eyes were on us. Dame had stopped laughing and chewed his food. His mom was looking back and forth between us, and I was trying not to make eye contact with her.

"Did y'all come here together?"

"No, ma'am."

"Don't no ma'am me after you just checked my son at my table like that."

"I'm sorry, that was just nasty for everybody to see all of his food."

"You're ok, chile. You beat me to it; hell, he know not to be doing that nasty shit at my table. Ohh boy, you got me cussing on my Father's day. Forgive me."

Destini started laughing and I did too; I couldn't hold it anymore. She reminded me a lot of Big Mama, and I know Karter could feel it too.

After everyone was done eating, the women cleared the table and Dez and Dame washed the dishes. I took a picture of it, and Dame got mad because I put it on Facebook.

Karter's fat ass was laid across a chaise asleep with Dez rubbing her scalp. These two acted like they had been together for years, but I loved it because my best friend was happy, and I was all for it.

I got my phone out and started ordering a bunch of pencil skirts, blazers, and button-downs. I was going to be on my full business swag for this job.

I looked up at Dame, and he was staring at me. He was looking good, but I wasn't trying to go there again. I saw that being with him would cause me to have to slap a few bitches, and I wasn't feeling that

Dame

Melodee had her face all into her phone, and I wanted to snatch it and see what she was looking at.

"What you over there looking at?"

"None of your business."

"Don't make me come over there and see for myself."

"Damn, I'm shopping, is that ok with you? Are you about to hand over that black card? Well, mind your business."

"Y'all fight like a married couple, G, shut up. Just fuck and make up already, pissing me off."

Destini was watching *Plug Love* on Amazon Video and was all into the TV. She turned the volume up on the TV more, and Dez snatched the remote from her and turned it back down.

"Nigga, you see she still sleep, why would you turn this shit up?"

"Maaann you better carry her ass to a bed. I ain't about to mute my damn show for Karter. That's my girl and all, but shit."

"Destini, you ain't shit, I can hear you. Can you start it over, though?"

Karter stood up, and Dez pulled her next to him with his arm was draped over her body. These niggas were the ones who acted like a married couple, if anything.

Melodee put her phone in her purse and stood up to go to the bathroom that was downstairs in the laundry room. I got up when she went inside and waited in the hallway until she was done. When the door opened, I pushed her back and locked the door behind me.

"Can you stop treating me like this?"

"Like what?" She sat down on the edge of the tub and folded her arms across her chest.

"Mel, you know I didn't tell that girl shit about us, I ain't that type of nigga."

"No, what I know is a person who didn't even know my name knew something that should've been between me and you. And, I know for a fact I didn't tell her shit."

"Muhfuckas heard, Mel! It ain't like we were quiet. Shit, I was tearing it up."

"Ok, goodbye, now it's my fault?"

"That's not what the fuck I'm saying, if you just listen! I didn't tell that bitch shit, that's not even some shit I'll do. What's between me and you is between me and you. I just need you to work with me, Mel. I don't know what the last nigga did, but I ain't him."

"Well, now we can't do anything because technically, I work for you now."

"Well, I'll fire yo ass."

"And I'll sue the shit outta you, Dame."

"Damn, you petty like that?"

"Very much so."

I helped her stand up and opened the door. Destini was standing there with her ear to the door and tried to play it off when we saw her.

"Your sister nosey as hell."

"Shit, I just tryna see how long y'all was gon' be. You know how mama is about her upstairs bathrooms."

"You sound dumb as hell, move." I pushed her to the side, and we walked back out to go finish the movie.

Karter was examining Melodee's appearance before she looked at me and did the same thing. These muhfuckas acted like we just be fucking every time we see each other.

***

It was Saturday night and, of course, I had to be in the club tonight because Dez took care of the beginning of week shit I hated to do.

This would be the first night I actually worked with Mel, and I ain't gon' lie, I was nervous as hell. She had been avoiding me for so long, but she didn't have a choice but to kick it with me.

It was only seven o'clock, but I came early so I could try to beat her in. To my surprise, her little blue Volvo was already parked in the lot.

I came in through the back door since it was the quickest way to her office. There were some people here cleaning and setting up for the crazy crowd we got every Saturday.

Knock

Knock

"Come in!"

I opened her door, and she was sitting behind a big black desk, smoking and reading over some papers. She looked up at me and set the papers down.

"How can I help you?"

"What you in here doing? You looking real official with that outfit on."

"I'm doing my job, what else?"

"I'm sure we don't pay you to get high."

"You don't know what my terms were, you weren't in the room."

"Aw, you on some bullshit. Come here right quick, though."

She stood up and smoothed her pencil skirt down. When she walked from behind her desk, I noticed she wasn't wearing shoes.

"You couldn't handle heels, huh?"

"Don't play with me, you haven't seen my shoe closet. I ain't want people thinking this a strip club when I came in the door with high heels on."

"If you got them kinda heels in your closet, you need to throw them bitches away ASAP."

She sat next to me and passed me her blunt, and I pulled her feet onto my lap so I could rub them.

"Why you come in here, Dame?"

"I just came to check on you and see how you adjusting."

"I'm sure your brother told you I was handling business in here."

She was right; he did tell me how Mel picked up on everything fast and was doing stuff that wasn't even in her job description.

"I wanted to see for myself, though."

"Ok, well now you see."

"You gon' stop avoiding me now?"

"I have not been—"

"It's a yes or no, that's all I want to hear."

"Yeah, even though I HAVEN'T been avoiding you."

"Aite, do some work. I ain't gone leave until you do so you won't have to be out alone."

"Ok, bye."

I passed the blunt back to her and stood up to leave, and she walked back around her desk and sat down. I walked off with a smile; this was a step in the right direction with her stubborn ass

Dezmund "Dez"

I had attempted to cook a fancy dinner for Karter, but that shit failed. Instead, I was making her a big ass burger. She was always dragging me to Matteson to go to Fuddruckers for a damn burger, so I figured she'd like it.

She texted me when she was at the gate, so I opened it and went to the door to greet her. She was struggling to get her bag out the car, so I jogged down the stairs to help her.

"Why you ain't just say you needed help?"

"Because, I got it in there by myself, so I could get it out by myself."

"Shut up and get in the house."

"Oohhh, it smell good in here, Dezzy. What you making?"

She took her shoes off and ran her fat ass to the kitchen. She took one of the fries off the plate and sat on the stool at the island.

"How was yo day?"

"Crazy, I'm trying to put together a fundraiser show, and I think I'm putting too much pressure on the little babies."

"Are they crying and shit?"

"No, not yet anyway."

"Well, they good. You know when kids get tired of doing something, they'll start acting a damn fool."

"You right, but yeah, that was my day."

"What's the fundraiser for?"

"To raise money to buy the studio. I'm still short a little."

"How much you need?"

"Like $20,000 to buy it."

"I got you."

"No, Dez."

"I said I got you. This is something you want to do and you seem passionate, so I got you."

"I hate when you throw your money around. I don't care about that shit. You know that, right?"

"Maaann, gone with that shit, ain't nobody said—"

"But, it's the shit you do! Just because I vent to you about something don't mean I want you to jump to my rescue."

"That sound dumb as fuck! If I got a solution for yo problem, I'm gon' solve it, fuck is you getting mad for?"

She huffed, stood up out the stool, and turned around like she was about to walk off. I reached out over the island and grabbed her. I pulled her back to me, and I felt her shoulders drop.

"Where you going?"

"Home, I just want to relax."

"Sit the fuck down and eat this burger I made. Just because you get in yo lil' feelings, you just gon' leave? That's kid shit, Karter. I'm a grown ass man. As a man, YOUR MAN, I'm going to help you out and buy the studio for you. Don't cause unnecessary drama for us, bae; we good, ok?"

"Okay."

She turned around and got on her tippy toes so I could give her a kiss. I smacked her hard on the ass, and she sat back in her seat. I gave her the plate with her food, and she bowed her head to say grace before she dug in.

"Damn, bae. This shit. Is good as fuck." Karter was smacking her lips and talking between every smack.

"Thank you, are you coming to Ma's house with me tomorrow?"

"No, I think I'm going to sleep in. I'm so tired. Tell her I said hey, though."

"Aite, that's cool, you can gone head and take your bath while I clean up down here."

Usually, around this time, I would be heading to the club, but Dame and Mel were holding it down instead. Me and Karter both had crazy schedules, but we were making it work. I had been asking her to move in, but she refuse to leave her house.

When I got to the bedroom, she was sitting in a chair in the middle of the room, wearing some little shorts, a tank top, and some socks that came up to her knees.

"What you in here doing?"

"I been working on this all day for you. Sit in the chair, and keep your arms at your side."

I did what she said, and she pulled a small speaker out her gym bag. The song started, and it sound like Tank. When the beat dropped, she bent down in front of my face, and my attention was stuck right there. I couldn't even hear the song anymore; all I saw was Karter's body. The way she was bending and moving her hips, I could've sworn I heard her say she wanted a baby.

When she came and sat on lap, I snatched her shirt off and started kissing all over her chest.

"You supposed to keep your hands to the side."

"I don't care, girl. I couldn't help it anymore."

I stood up with her legs still wrapped around me, and pinned her against the wall. Whoever said high sex was the best sex was telling the absolute truth. I think I set a record tonight.

When we finally got done, it was past midnight, and Karter could barely keep her eyes open.

"Bae, you should have a class to teach bitches how to do that. I guarantee they niggas would stop cheating."

"But, then it'll be more women that can do what I just did for you."

"Naw baby, ain't nothing like the original. You ain't got nothing to worry about."

She gave me a kiss on the lips and got comfortable on her pillow. As always, she was asleep at the drop of a dime, and I turned on TV and watched Sports Center on mute.

The next morning, I got up and get dressed to go to Ma's house as always.

"Awww, where's Karter at?"

"She was tired, Ma. She said hey, though."

"You sure you ain't scare her off?"

"Dang Ma, that's how you feel?"

"I mean, baby, I didn't think I'd ever see the day when you actually fell in love with somebody."

"Who said anything about being in love?" I wasn't denying it, because I knew I loved Karter.

"You didn't have to say nothing; you can tell by the way you look at her, and the way you pay attention to her needs. I almost cried when I saw you rubbing her head when she was asleep. I'm proud of you."

"For what?"

"Opening up and giving somebody the chance to see the real you. I heard some crazy stories about you, even at eleven and twelve years old. I was scared the streets was going to take my baby away from me. I know you haven't been a baby in a long time, but you'll forever be my baby."

"Hey Ma, yo favorite daughter is here."

"You her only daughter, nigga, shut up."

Destini and Dame came walking in the house, disturbing the heart to heart I was having with my mama.

"Dame, stop always saying that *damn nigga* word! You make me whoop yo giant ass. Look, every time you bring yo ass over here, I end up cursing, get out my face."

Dame was standing in foyer holding his arms out like he ain't know what he did.

"Where Karter at?"

"Damn, everybody gon' ask me that like we always together?"

"Shiiiit, y'all are, but it's cool. Sis a good look for you."

"Thanks, Destini."

We ate and sat around watching a *Martin* marathon. I was texting Karter all day, and she had me ready to skip the food and come back home.

Can you pleeeeaasseeee bring me a plate of whatever Ma cooked

What you gon' do for it?

Nothing lol

*Guess you ain't hungry *two finger emoji**

Ok, ok I'll do whatever you want

Marry me?

Don't play like that, Dezmund

I'm dead ass serious

Ok

Ok what?

Yea, I'll marry you

Aite, I'll see you when I get home

"Look at Dez uglass ass over there smiling like a princess." Destini smacked me in the back of the head, and I threw a pillow at her.

"Destini, keep playing and Imma knock you out like the man you think you are."

Damn bro, that hurts." She held her chest like she was really in pain.

"Ma!"

"What, boy?"

"I'm thinking about marrying Karter."

"Oh, shit."

Dame's eyes got big, and he was staring at me like he was trying to see if I was serious.

"If you're serious about this girl and believe she is the one, then I'm all for it."

"Thank you, Ma."

"Dame, run with me right quick."

I ran to Chicago Ridge Mall and went to the first jewelry store I saw.

"Welcome to Rogers & Hollands, was there something specific you were looking for today?"

"Yeah, an engagement ring."

"Well, congratulations, do you know the ring size?"

"Naw, hold on."

What's your ring size?

6

"A six."

"Ok, do you have a price range?"

"Naw, it don't matter."

I scanned the display case until I found the perfect ring.

"Give me that one."

"Ok, that one is going to cost you over $20,000."

"Bi—ma'am, I don't care about the price, I want that one."

"Ok, I'll be right back with you."

"Bro, you was about to spazz in the bitch. I was gon' go crazy with you and grab that watch."

"Nigga, you been around Melodee too long."

"Man, she don't be stealing, she just nosey as hell. I watched her ass check every door in that bitch, TWICE!"

"Damn, you be stalking, bro?"

"Hell yeah, gotta make sure she don't be having no niggas in there. I gotta holla at UPS, though, they need a new delivery driver. She order too much shit for him to keep coming back."

I just shook my head and got my bag from the lady ringing me out. He followed me back to the car, still talking about how Melodee be curving him. I wished she would just stop playing with him so he could shut the hell up.

Karter

"What do you mean you getting married, Karter?"

I called Melodee after Dez texted me about my ring size. At first, I thought he was playing when he asked me that, but he was dead serious. Crazy part about it is, I was actually happy and couldn't wait to become Mrs. Wright.

"He texted me and asked me to marry him, so I said yeah."

"You pregnant, bitch?"

"Nooo, Melodee, damn."

"What the hell was I supposed to think? It's been all of a month and a half, and you already talking about marrying him? This some book shit— which one of the heffas in them books encouraged this? How do you know this feeling will last?"

"I don't, but you only live once. It's not like we getting married tomorrow. I just accepted his text proposal."

"Well, you know I'll be there with bells and whistles, just give me a date."

"Thank you, bestie."

"You're welcome, babe, but let me go find something to eat. I don't appreciate you abandoning me like this."

"You act like you can't cook, Mel, stop it."

"I don't feel like doing all that. I just want to eat. I think I'm going to Red Lobster."

"Bye, lazy."

We hung up and I laid across the sectional, catching up on the episodes of *Love and Hip Hop* I recorded on his DVR.

Dez came halfway through my second episode, so I paused it and sat up so I could get my plate.

"My bad I took so long, I know yo fat ass starving to death. I better still have some flaming hots in there. I see them red ass finger tips."

"Shut up, I brought them here anyway."

I snatched the Tupperware out of his hand, and my mouth was watering from smelling all the food. I stuck my fork in the macaroni first, and Dez threw a box down next to me. I started smiling big and was about to open it, until I stopped myself and stood up.

"Hold on, let me go wash my hands, You let me start eating barbecue and wanna do this." I ran to the bathroom and closed the door. I washed my hands and put on lotion. I couldn't have ashy hands with my ring. I attempted to fix my ponytail, and Dez banged on the door.

"Come on, Karter, I ain't about to be waiting all night."

"Wait, Dez!"

I took a deep breath and opened the bathroom door. Dez was right outside the door on one knee."

"Is this a better proposal?"

"Yes."

I pulled his face to mine and gave him a long kiss on the lips. He put the ring on my finger, and my breath was taken away from the beautiful, cushion-cut diamond ring.

Dez stood up, and I walked back to the living room to get my phone. I took a picture to send to Melodee, and she responded right away.

Daaammn! Ok, I wanna be like u when I grow up!

I start taking more pictures, showing off my ring, and Dez snatched my phone from me. I did some poses and Dez laughed while he took the picture.

"You wanna take a picture with me?"

"Nah bae, that's yo thang. I don't want my face out there like that."

"Come ooonnnn, people gon' think I bought myself a ring."

"So, fuck them."

"We don't even have any pictures together, period." I sat down with my lip poked out, and Dez slapped my thigh and sat down next to me.

"You a cry baby, take the picture."

"Stop playing with me."

"I'm not, yet."

I tried to get both of us in the frame, and I couldn't.

"Yo short ass arms gon' cut me out the picture."

He took the phone back, and I instructed him on the different angles to do. We ended up with thirty pictures, and I picked my favorite five to post on Facebook. I was barely on here, but I had over 1,300 friends. Most of them were people I went to high school and college with.

I kept the caption on our photos short and sweet, and within minutes, it was blowing up from likes and comments.

"Bae, our picture just went live, look."

"That's cuz yo man fine as fuck, girl. Now, move around so I can buss Dame ass with my boa Lebron." He got up and turned his Xbox One on, so I connected my phone to his Bluetooth speaker and had Nicki Minaj radio playing. I finished eating my food and laughing at the comments on my post from Destini and Melodee.

****

Monday morning, I was up early to meet the owner of the dance studio. Mr. Rice was a cool guy. His wife was the one that opened the studio, but he took over once she got sick.

"Hey there, little Karter, how you doing this morning?"

"I'm good, Mr. Rice. I came to make my offer for the studio."

"I was wondering when you was going to come and see me. What you got for me?"

"I have $15,000 in cash, and I can write you a check for whatever extra I'm short. I know the post said $40,000, but this is where the negotiation kicks in."

"How about this, make the check out for another $15,000, and I'll take care of whatever changes you want to make? You just have to the painting yourself, or hire someone."

"Thank you so much, I have everything right now."

I handed him the envelope from my bag and wrote him a check for twenty thousand. I knew he was moving to a nursing facility out of state, and I wanted to make sure they were well taken care of.

I did a quick walkthrough and noted anything I was changing before I left and headed to Menards to buy paint and the other materials I needed.

When I left there, I ran to Save A Lot on 107th and Halsted, so I could grab some stuff for dinner. I had just loaded the car when somebody walked up behind me and pushed the cart into my legs.

"What the hell?"

I was pushed against my truck, and a tall man was standing behind me with his hood pulled over his head.

"You should pay attention to your surroundings, especially with the company you keep."

He turned to run off, and my heart was beating a mile a minute. I hopped in the car and pulled out of the lot quickly. I circled the block a few times to make sure no one was following me home, then I pulled into the garage I never used. I entered the kitchen from the garage door, and I put all my bags down on the floor.

I pulled my phone out and called Dez.

"Yo?"

"Um, where are you?"

"Making some runs for the club, wassup?"

"Something kind of just happened, but I don't want you to start acting crazy and stuff ok?"

"What happened, Karter?"

"A guy walked up on me when I was at the grocery store and—"

"What he look like?"

"I don't know, Dez, he had a hoodie on."

"So, you see a nigga with a hood on, early as hell, and you don't think to move around?"

"I didn't see him! I was putting bags in the trunk."

"Go to my house, and wait for me."

"No, I'm at home, you come here when you're done."

"Bet."

He hung up, so I put up the groceries and start prepping my catfish. I heard someone banging at the door when I was in the middle of cooking, so I ran to open it before I went back to the kitchen.

"Fuck is you just opening the door for?"

"I knew it was you."

"How? You ain't check, you just gon' open it and leave like you like in Pleasantville or some shit."

"Please don't start with that, gimme a kiss."

"What you in here cooking anyway?"

"Catfish, greens, candied yams, my macaroni in the oven, and my cornbread just got out."

"I'm telling Ma you tryna compete with her."

"No I'm not, shut up."

"Aite, but we need to talk about you moving in."

"Not gon' happen."

"Why not?"

"We had a whole conversation about this before. I'm not leaving Big Mama's house, you can move in here."

"It's not enough space, Karter, how Imma fit all my shit? You want me to expand some walls in here?"

"We can do that; the living room don't need to be that big."

"Listen to yourself, baby, that's unnecessary. Just think about what I said. I'll be back when I close up, aite?

"Ok, just call and wake me up before you leave. Be safe."

"I got you."

Melodee

"Oh my God, you cooked for me? Yeessss. Now, what you over there looking crazy for?"

I had just walked in the house from shopping, and went right to the kitchen to wash my hands and eat.

"Dez, he wants me to move with him."

"Ok soooo, do he want you to move into a cardboard box?"

"No, into his house."

"Girl, you if don't pack yo shit and get out. That man done bought you a car, proposed to you, and you moping around because he want you to move into a damn mansion? Let me call him, shit, I'll move in."

"You should be the last one to talk. Aren't you still running from Dame?"

"That's different."

"How?"

"We not talking about me right now."

"Thought so."

She went in her room, and I sat down to look at the club footage on my iPad. It didn't have sound, but I saw Dame just sitting in his office with his feet kicked up. I sent him a text from his phone to see his reaction.

Hey, what you doing after you close?

He jumped up out his chair, and I start laughing.

Why shorty, you miss me?

Yeah, you gon' come over tonight?

He looked directly up at the camera and smiled.

I'll be there.

I was just horny, so I hope he ain't think this was something other than that. Dame was cool, but I didn't think I was ready to open myself up like that again.

I hung up my new clothes and went to take a long bubble bath. The nights at the club were long, but I could honestly say I enjoyed it. I'd been trying to get some celebrities to come through. So far, I haven't been lucky, but I wasn't giving up.

I ended up dozing off in the bath, and didn't wake up until I heard Karter banging on my room door.

"I know you heard me! You could've put the food up!"

"Shut uuuppp, Kay."

"Dame is on his way, they closed it down. Some niggas tried to bring a gun in there. I know you getting ready for daddy."

I snatched the door open with my towel wrapped around my body, and she took off running.

"Grow up, Karter!" I slammed my door and rubbed my body down with my Jergens.

By the time I was dressed in my cami and Victoria's Secret pajama pants, I heard Dame's loud voice in the living room.

"Mel, bring yo ass out here, you ain't sleep!"

I came out my room and was on Facebook Live, recording.

"Fuck you doing?" Dame got in the camera and started licking his lips in the camera.

"I'm sexy as hell, boooaa. What's that shit popping on the screen?"

"People laughing at yo ugly ass."

"Naw, them hearts, bro. You a hater. What that say? Damn, what's his name?

He was about to start talking to the camera, until I ended the live feed. I went to the kitchen and sat my phone on the island so I could get some ice cream.

"Damn, sis; you being petty?"

"Dez, shut up; don't be instigating."

"Bae, you know I don't want nobody but you." Dame put his arm around me, and I pushed him off me.

"Baby mama be tripping, I'll get her right."

"Y'all ass crazy, bro. Mel, you taking care of all the morning business, you can't close no more."

"Shiiiit, don't threaten me with a good time."

I took my ice cream to my room, and Dame was right behind me.

"Why you keep playing with me, bae?"

"How am I playing?"

"You know what, I ain't playing this game no mo. When you done being on that bullshit, you know how to find me."

He walked out my room and I heard the front door close. My phone lit up, and it was Karter texting me.

Y'all just left?

He did, said he was done playing with me

Mel...

Goodnight, bestie

I wasn't going to be all butt hurt over this. If Dame wasn't strong enough to handle me, then oh well.

Karter

It had been a month since I officially owned the dance studio, and I loved every minute of it. I was able to come in whenever I wanted to and just rehearse, or dance to let off steam; it was perfect.

I still hadn't officially moved into Dez's house, but I was definitely here more than I was at home.

"Dez! Bae, you home?"

I was walking through the house and I didn't see him anywhere; all his cars were outside, so I figured Dame must've picked him up. Lately, he had been moving differently and I was worried. Last week, he snuck out the house when he thought I was asleep, and was dressed in all black. I didn't say anything because I was actually afraid to know the answer. The last thing I wanted was for Dez to get into some kind of trouble.

I went to the kitchen to find something to eat, and I was scrolling through Facebook. My ex, Malik, had been liking all my pictures, and I was thinking about blocking him. We ended on bad terms because he had a temper, and he was definitely in my past.

I was laid across the couch reading when Dez came stomping through the house and was going straight to his basement.

"Well, hello to you too."

His hand went to his waist, and I jumped up off the couch so he could see me.

"My bad, bae, I didn't even know you was here."

"My car is right outside."

"I wasn't paying attention. I'll be back."

He unlocked the basement and went down there. Sometimes, I wanted to get on my Melodee shit and go snooping, but Dez' ass is kind of crazy. I got up so I could get started on dinner, and Dez was coming back upstairs at the same time.

"When we gon' start having babies?" He wrapped his arms around my waist and kissed me on my neck.

"I don't know, we're not even married yet."

"We could go get married right now, baby."

"I mean, I know I don't have family, but I do want to plan this out."

"I ain't mean it like that, baby. We could just start our own family."

"I'm not ready to start having babies yet."

"I'm damn near thirty, and you ain't too far behind."

"That doesn't mean I'm ready to have kids, Dezmund."

"Well, I ain't been pulling out, so you might be pregnant already."

"That's exactly why I take my birth control pill every day, faithfully."

"Where they at? I'll throw them bitches in the trash where they belong."

"Get out my kitchen being irritating."

"Aite, what you cooking?"

"Whatever I cook, you're gonna eat it."

"You know I clean my plate, baby!"

I cooked us steak, mashed potatoes, and fried asparagus, and Dez ate like he had been starved for days.

I was taking a long, hot shower when I felt Dez creeping into the shower behind me.

"Since you not gon' give me a baby, we can practice, right?"

I was lifted off my feet, and he entered me slowly while he held me against the shower wall. One thing I would never deny was my fiancé's pipe game. Shiiiit, I'd marry him just for that dick.

***

I was getting my morning Iced Caramel Latte from Dunkin Donuts on 87th and the Dan Ryan, when I noticed an old school Chevy whip into the parking lot, and Malik hopped out. It was like I spoke his existence up; he swaggered over to me, and I had to roll my eyes.

"Damn, that's how it is now, Karter?"

"Um, yeah. Excuse me, I gotta go."

"Hold the fuck on."

He snatched me by my arm, and I had to look at him like he was crazy.

"Get your fucking hands on me. I see you still didn't learn your lesson."

"Bitch, who you talking to? I'll kill yo ass out here and won't blink twice. I see that nigga you been posting too. I don't give a fuck. If he want problems, bring him my way."

Malik was choking the life outta me, and I ended up dropping my cup and spilling it all on my shoes.

"Get your hands off her! I'm calling the cops!" An older guy was yelling at Malik, and he threw me to the ground before he ran back in his car and sped off.

"Are you ok, Miss?"

He helped me off the ground as I was trying to control my breathing.

"Yes, I am, thank you."

He walked away, and I got in my car to go home and change.

I cursed when I saw Melodee walking out the door because I knew she was going to snap.

"Hey boo, shouldn't you be opening the— WHAT THE FUCK HAPPENED TO YOUR NECK?"

She snatched my arm and damn near dragged me into the house.

"Malik, his crazy ass snapped. I was literally walking from Dunkin Donuts, and he pulled up me."

"His ass ain't learn from the last time, huh?"

"That's what I said!"

The day I left Malik, he called himself hitting me, and I called Melodee to come get me. She came in the house on charge, and we ended up jumping him. I'm talking about Mel had a steel Louisville slugger and went to town on him.

"You tell Dez?"

"No, girl Dez is a freaking psychopath, I'm scared."

"Fuck that, I'm calling him."

"Please don't!"

"Yo?"

I heard Dez's voice on the phone, and my heart dropped. I was so mad at Melodee for calling him. I was just going to stay home for a few days.

"I think you need to get over here."

"What's going on, sis?"

"Karter."

That was all she was able to get out before he hung up. I knew he was going to lose his shit when he saw me. I changed out of my dirty clothes and put on a plain tan tank and some jeans. I heard banging at the door and had to do some deep breathing. I stayed in my room because I didn't want Mel to witness whatever he was going to do.

"Where she at?"

"In her room."

"Aite."

I heard his big feet stomping down the hall before my door came flying open.

"What's going on?"

"Nothing."

"So, why Mel call me over here, and why you looking at the floor?" He lifted my head, and his eyebrows furrowed.

"That wasn't there when you left the house this morning."

I sighed, "I know, Dez. Can you sit down, please?"

He kicked his shoes off and sat on the edge of my bed. I stood up and started pacing until he grabbed my wrist and pulled me between his legs.

"Talk to me, Bugs?"

"Um. My ex pulled up on me when I was leaving from getting my caffeine, and he choked me."

"Fuck he choke you for?"

"I don't fucking know, Dez, he's crazy. It's not like I told him to choke the shit outta me. It took an old man saying he called the police for him to let me go."

I saw a distant look in Dez's eyes, and I grabbed his face. "Please don't do nothing crazy. Look at me, Dez. Please?"

He didn't say anything, and yet he said so much. The look I read in his eyes screamed murder.

"Just come back to me every night, please?"

"You gon' move in?"

"Yes, Dez. fine."

Dezmund "Dez"

I was laying in Karter's little ass bed, and I was on a thousand. She really had me fucked up if she thought I wasn't going to get at dude. The second she went to sleep, I got up and left out the room.

When I went to the living room, Mel was sitting on the couch dressed in all camouflage

"Fuck you doing, G.I. Jane?"

"Shit, we 'bout to go get that nigga."

"Nahhh, I'm good. I got my right-hand man already."

"Well nigga, I could be yo left. That's my sister, and I'm not going."

"That's my future wife, trust me, nobody want this nigga dead more than me. But, I'm the one that's gon' do it."

"Thank you."

"For what?"

"Loving Karter. I didn't think I'll ever see her happy again."

"Aw, that's forever, you ain't gotta worry about her. Tell her I'll be back to pick her up."

"Aite, be safe."

I walked out the door and called Dame as soon as I got in the car.

"Whatcho goof ass want?"

"Meet me at my house, now."

"Bet."

I didn't have to say much; my brother knew when I was playing, and when shit was serious. Wight now, this shit real fucking serious.

Dame was pulling up at the same time I was, so we entered the gate together. We both parked our cars and went to the Monte Carlo I kept dipped off. I ain't want niggas to see my regular whip and know I was coming.

"So, what happened?" Dez finally spoke as we were in the car driving down 95th street.

"You know a nigga name Malik?"

"From 87th?"

"Yeah. Nigga put his hand on my girl, I'm 'bout to go see 'bout him."

"No doubt."

We pulled up to the Five Star Liquors on 87th and Sangamon, and I spotted him standing against the building, laughing like shit was sweet.

"We killing this nigga out here?"

"Nah, I just want him to know it's coming."

I tied my wheat Timbs up and we got out the car at the same time. When the small crowd heard our doors close, they all turned around squinting, trying to see who we were.

"Damn, them the Wright brothers, I thought they was out the game?" somebody tried to whisper as we were passing by, but we heard that shit.

"Ay, you Malik?"

"Who want to know?"

This ugly, rat-looking nigga had the nerve to smirk at me. Dame reached for his steel, but I put my hand up, signaling him that I had it. I handed Dame my gun, and I hit Malik right in his mouth.

"DAAAMMMNNN!!"

He stumbled and hit the brick wall behind him before he was able to recover and stand up straight.

"Damn, what the fuck was that for? I don't even know y'all."

"Obviously not, you put your hands on my wife."

The people that were standing around were now walking away. I guess my reputation precedes me.

"You ain't got shit to say now, huh?"

"Come on, Dez, I was just playing with her, I barely touched her."

"Aw, so you do know me, huh? Good, I'll be back for you, so I advise you to get the fuck moving."

I turned to walk off, and Dame stopped me. "Hell naw, he ain't getting away that easy."

Dame shot Malik in the hand and walked back to the car with Malik screaming like a bitch behind us.

"You letting him live, g? I know you ain't turning soft on me?"

"Fuck you, I did it for Karter. She don't need to see that side of me."

"I'm proud of you, man, you growing up."

"Yeah, follow suit, nigga."

"I ain't got no girl, yet. I met a lil' shorty the other day I forgot to hit up."

"Aite, keep playing and Melodee gon' turn up on yo ass."

"She still playing, so I'm good on her."

I drove him to pick his car up from my house, and then I drove to pick Karter up.

"Dez?"

"Wassup, bae?"

"What did you do?"

"Nothing."

"Are you lying?"

"No Karter, damn. I ain't gotta lie about shit."

"Don't get all snappy with me, Dezmund. I'm only trying to protect you."

"Man, I'm good, I can handle myself."

"But, what if something happened to you? What am I supposed to do then? You'll make me live without you because of something you handled yourself?"

I couldn't say shit. I was just staring at her as we lay in bed.

"I promise you, I ain't going nowhere."

Melodee

Man, ever since Dame walked out the house that night, it seemed like he had gotten sexier overnight. His beard was thicker, those big juicy pink lips were looking extra scrumptious, and he had got his hair cut a little lower than normal. I was ready to give in to temptation, then he'd do something that would have me like, *nope forget it*. Like now, he had the nerve to bring a woman to the club on the night we were closing together.

When I saw that mess he walked in the front door with, I had to laugh, like real loud. I don't know who she was trying to impress with a too-little dress and too much makeup. Definitely a clown, in my eyes.

I was called down to the bar, so I stood up and fixed my midi pencil skirt before I walked down the hall to the main stairway.

"Ay, Mel!"

I tried to make it past Dame's office without him seeing me, but it was a fail. I stepped back to his door and folded my arms across my breast.

"Mel, this is Sonya. Sonya, this is the club manager, Mel."

"It's Melodee."

I turned back around and walked away from his door and headed down to the bar, like I started to in the first place. He had a lot of fucking nerve trying to show off that bitch in my face; let the shoe be on the other foot, though.

"Melodee, this guy wants to complain about the food."

Kim, the bartender, pointed to a guy sitting at the end of the bar. I shook off my previous attitude and got into professional mode.

"Hi, I'm Melodee, the manager here at Promise. What seems to be the problem today?"

"Shiiiit, these wings was nasty, who y'all got cooking back there?"

I looked down at his tray of hot wings, and he only had three out of ten left, but he claimed they were nasty.

"Well, seeing as though you ate more than half, I can guarantee you were enjoying them, but if you just wanted some more, I got you."

I put an order in for another 10 wings for him, then walked back to my office. This time, Dame's door was closed and I smiled. I sat back behind my desk and finished my paperwork.

Knock

Knock

"Come in!"

Dame walked into my office, and I rolled my eyes.

"How can I help you?"

"That was rude as fuck. You hurt her feelings, yo, she just left."

"I don't give a fuck, you better be lucky it was only her feelings that got hurt. Now, if you're not in here about club business, you can leave."

"Fuck is yo problem? You don't want me, so what you mad fo?"

"I missed the part of that sentence that was about the club?"

"You got me fucked up, bro."

I stood up and started gathering all my stuff and putting it in my bag. Dame was still standing up, and he was watching my every move.

I put my loafers back on my feet and pushed past him.

"You just gon' leave?"

"Yes, now get out so I can lock my office."

He left and went down the stairs to the main floor, and I took the back stairs that led me to my car. I threw my stuff in the backseat and was getting ready to pull off.

POW! POW! POW!

I heard about ten gunshots, and I threw my car back in park and ran back into the club. People were running all over, trying to get out the door, and it look like a stampede of animals. I ran to Dame's office and he wasn't in there. My heart started beating fast as I took out my phone and dialed his number. It went to voicemail three times, so I ran down the stairs to look for him.

"Dame! Damien! Kim, you seen Dame?"

"They shot him! H-he stumbled towards the bathroom." Kim was shaking, and I almost tripped over my own feet running to the bathroom.

There was a blood trail leading to the men's bathroom, and I saw smeared bloody prints on the door.

I called Karter, and she answered on the first ring.

"Hello?"

"Just wait, something happened at the club."

"What? What happened at the club?"

"Where bro at? What happened?"

I heard Dez and Karter both talking at the same time as I entered the bathroom.

"OH MY GOD! DAME! He's bleeding everywhere! What am I supposed to do?"

I dropped to knees where Dame was laid out by the sink, and I was looking over his body, trying to see where he was hurt.

"Mel! Call an ambulance, we on the way. Find where he's hit and apply pressure. Please don't let my brother die, Mel."

Dez hung up the phone, and I swear my heart stopped. If Dame died right now, I'd feel like shit. That was not what I wanted our last memories to be.

"911, what's your emergency?"

"There was a shooting at Club Promise. My name is Melodee Golden, I'm the manager here, and we need an ambulance now. The owner is shot, we're in the men's bathroom."

"Is he conscious?"

"I mean yes, but no, he's going in and out."

"Try to get him to stay conscious, the paramedics are three minutes out."

"Ok."

I noticed he was holding his neck, so I took my button up off and replaced his hand with my shirt.

"Dame, look at me, you better not fucking die. I swear I will be so mad at you."

He smiled a little, and I felt a tear roll down my cheek. Dame reached up and wiped my tear, which caused more tears to fall.

The door was opened, and I saw the paramedics rush in with a stretcher.

"Ma'am, you have to move back so we can do our job."

"It's his neck, I don't want to let it go."

"You did great, my partner here is going to take over and hold his neck. Just stand up slowly and move your hand after he takes over."

I did what he said, and they took over to get him transferred on the stretcher, and they were rushing out the door to the ambulance.

I ran out the door to my car and followed them to the hospital. We made it to Christ Hospital, and I grabbed my purse before I ran to the emergency room. Doctors and nurses were running around, and I tried to find somebody to help me. I finally found the receptionist desk, and I hoped she had some information for me.

"I'm looking for Damien Wright, they just brought him in, he was shot."

"If they just brought him in, he's not in the system yet. I can give you the clipboards to fill out what you know about him so they won't call him John Doe."

I grabbed the papers from her and texted Kim so she could lock the club.

I need you to stay until the last person is gone, and lock up. There's a spare key in Dame's top drawer. I'll send you the temporary alarm code. Remember, there are cameras everywhere!!

I got you, Melodee, lol

I sat with my leg bouncing, trying to write everything I knew about Dame on this paper. I heard a bunch a commotion at the front door before I heard Karter's voice.

"Dez, slow down please, and calm down."

"Karter!"

She looked at me, and her eyes were wide and they started to water. I forgot I was covered in Dame's blood.

"Is he ok? What happened?"

"I don't know. I left out the back because we had a stupid ass argument, and when I was pulling off, I heard the gunshots. I jumped out the car and ran looking for him, and Kim just kept saying they shot him and he ran to the bathroom. I took off and found him on the floor. He had lost so much blood, but he was still looking at me. He smiled right before the paramedics made it and brought it here. Please don't let him die, oh my God."

I couldn't hold it in anymore. I broke down crying on the floor, and Karter sat on the floor with me, rubbing my back.

"Sissy, it's not your fault, don't blame yourself just because y'all had a small argument. I know you and Dame been playing, but when he comes home, y'all gon get y'all shit together. No more running from him, Melodee, let him love you."

"You just had to make this about us being together."

"Yeah, I knew it would get you to think about something else. We gotta be strong for Dame, and Dez."

"What happened to my baby, Dezmund?!"

We looked up to see their mother and Destini rushing toward us. I stood up and wiped my face. She looked at me, and covered her both with her hands.

"Mel, what happened?"

"Somebody shot him; from what I saw, he was bleeding from his neck."

Dez was pacing the floor, and Karter was walking right beside him, trying to get him to stop.

"Mel, check it out right quick."

Dez pulled me to the side, and I was scared he was going to bruise my arm, but I knew he wasn't doing it on purpose.

"I need you to check the cameras, from every angle. Slow motion, if you have to. I need to see a face. Was anybody else hurt?"

"I don't even know, I ran out so fast."

"I need you to go back to the club."

"No, I'm waiting on the fucking doctors."

"Listen!"

His voice was stern, so I shut up really quick.

"You need to go change anyway; go take a shower and come right back. You can watch the videos on your phone, or the tablet."

"Ok, please call me if I'm not back and they say something."

"I got you."

I gave everyone a hug and walked out the door. The twenty-minute drive to the club was the worst. I think I cried the whole way there, but I had to let the rest of the tears go.

When I walked into the club, the last detective was leaving. Kim was at the bar with a cup in her hands, and she tried to hurry up and put it down when she saw me.

"Don't worry, I'll take it out your check."

I handed her the five hundred dollars I had in my wallet, and she left out the front door after I took the keys from her.

I walked around, making sure the club was completely empty before I went to my office. The club was trashed, and I know the police probably did some of this.

I grabbed my Adidas track suit and walked to the full bathroom I had in my office. This was the main reason I told Dez I wanted this one; it had a shower in it.

The water rinsed all the blood off me, and I just watched it go down the drain. I couldn't believe how this night ended. I felt like I was trapped in the Twilight Zone or some shit.

I heard my phone ringing, and I almost broke my neck trying to jump out the shower.

"Hello?"

"Yes, this is Detective Normal. I'm working the case of the shooting, and I'm trying to get a copy of the security footage."

"Hello ma'am; unfortunately, the cameras aren't working. We recently switched systems, so everything isn't set up."

"Are you sure?"

"Yeah, isn't that what I just said?"

"I understand this is a trying time for you, but I'm just trying to do my job."

"Ok, well I'm sorry I can't help you do your job, officer."

"Detective."

"Same thing; you can interview the bartender. She's the only one who was up front to see everything. Now, I have to go."

I threw my clothes on, and grabbed my iPad before I left back out the door. When I made it back to the hospital, everyone was still sitting around waiting. I found an empty corner and plugged the iPad up to charge. I signed into the system and watched everything that happened. When I saw Dame get shot, I wanted to throw up. The person who shot him was moving fast, so I couldn't see it at first. Just as I found the perfect frame to see who it was, I just shook my head and stood up to tell Dez.

"Family of Damien Wright?"

"Yes?"

We all stood up, and he led us to a private family room.

"I'm Dr. Morris, the doctor that worked on Mr. Wright. As you may know, he was shot multiple times, and we might have to give him a blood transfusion. The shots that were in his shoulder went in and out, but I still had to do some repairs. Now, this is where it gets tricky."

He put some X-rays up and was pointing different stuff to us.

"He was shot in the neck, and it seems a little fragment is still there. I'll have to go in to get it, and even though it is a serious operation, I am extremely confident in my ability to get the job done."

"Is he going to be ok?"

"Absolutely; it might be uncomfortable for him to speak for a few weeks, but he'll recover just fine."

"Ok, do whatever you have to do to help my baby."

"I will, ma'am. There's a waiting room upstairs closer to the trauma level, and it's a private room."

He led us upstairs, and everybody picked a recliner chair to lay in, but of course, Dez and Karter laid on the couch together.

I closed my eyes and tried to think of anything but Dame's bloody body.

Dame

Beep...Beep...beep

I tried to open my eyes, but it felt like these bitches was glued shut. When I finally opened them all the way, I was in a hospital bed, and all the lights were off except the light from the TV.

I saw Melodee stretched out in a recliner, and Dez was holding Karter like a damn baby while he sat in another recliner. Those two be irritating as hell sometimes, but I'm glad I was still here to see it. I tried to talk, but I had a tube in my throat. I hit my hand on the bed rail, and Melodee was the first one up.

She hit my call button, and a nurse came running in the room.

"He's up, get this shit out his throat."

"Ok, let me go get the doctor; just relax, Mr. Wright."

She ran off out the door, and I was looking at Melodee, smiling the best I could anyway. She looked at me and start smiling back at me.

"Shut up, I know you thinking something crazy."

Melodee had me feeling like Dez. I was ready to marry her ass. I remember the look in her eyes before I passed out. She could keep fighting me off if she wanted, but I ain't going nowhere.

"Good to see you up, Mr. Wright. I'm just going to do a quick look over, then I'll get that tube out of you." The nurse took my blood pressure and temperature as the doctor was shining the light in my face.

"Follow the light for me. Ok, great. Now, I'm going to run the back of my pen down your body, let me know if you feel it."

He took the pen from the top of my head, all the way down to my toes. He did it again to the other side and wrote something on a clipboard.

"Grab both my hands and squeeze as hard as you can."

I did what he said, and I squeezed extra tight on purpose.

"Whew, you got quite a grip there. Ok, this is going to be uncomfortable for about five seconds."

He washed his hands and put on some gloves, and the nurse stood right next to him holding a small basin. When he pulled the tube out my throat, I wanted to punch the shit out of him.

"You have some fresh ice water over there. Drink it slow; it might burn, but that's normal. We'll be checking on you regularly, but don't hesitate to call if you need us."

I just nodded at him and he left out the room, along with the nurse.

"Where my mama at?" My voice sounded hoarse as hell, but oh well.

"We sent her and Destini home, it's like six in the morning."

"How are you feeling?"

Mel was staring at neck and arm that was wrapped in a big ass bandage, and in a sling.

"I'm good bae, damn. You getting on my nerves already."

"Ok, you know what, that's why you going home alone."

"I'm glad y'all asses can stop acting fucking weird."

"Shut up, Karter."

Melodee held my straw so I could take a drink out of my cup, and the cold water was feeling good as hell going down my throat

"We gon' go get some sleep. Mama at yo house since it's closer. I'll holla at you later, bro."

"Aite, that's cool."

Him and Karter left, and Mel start letting out the couch so she could lay down.

"You don't wanna lay with me? it's enough room for yo little ass."

"Boy, I'm thick, stop hating."

"You ain't thick yet, but I'll help you with that all day."

"Can you recover first? Dang."

"Girl, I'm good, you just gon' have to do all the work for a minute."

"Soooo. I know who did it."

"I know who did too, I saw the niggas. I got this handled over here, baby girl."

She got close to me and laid her head on my good arm. I wasn't gon' stress the shit now because unless them niggas left Earth all together, I was gon' see them real soon.

I was able to go to sleep for another few hours before nurses came in fucking with me. Melodee didn't wake up when they came to check my bandages, so they had to work around her.

Mama walked in, and she just shook her head.

"If you ever do that again, Damien Katrell Wright, Imma kill you myself."

"Damn Og, that's how you feel? It ain't like I wanted to get shot, shit hurts."

"Well, you should've shot they ass back."

I start laughing, and Melodee finally woke up, looking confused.

"'Bout time you got up, they couldn't even do they job with yo big head ass all in the way."

"Hey Ma, I'm not even gon' respond to your son and his foolishness."

Dez and Karter came into the room, and she looked half sleep.

"Damn sis, you good?"

"Yeah, I just been up for a long time."

"Cuz yo ass was tryna watch me. I told you I wasn't leaving back out the house."

"Yeah, well Dezmund. When you're pacing the floor and putting a hole in the carpet, I tend to not believe you."

Karter was rolling her eyes, and me and Ma were staring at her shocked. Dez pushed Karter to sit down in the by the window, and he stood behind her.

"I ain't think y'all even had arguments. I thought Karter was a little scary one."

"Ma, I told you, she be spazzing on me when we're alone. She got all y'all fooled like she just sooo innocent. Nah, she crazy."

"Don't lie on me." She hit Dez in the stomach, and we all laughed at them.

"I see we got the whole clan in here. Well, so far, everything's is looking good. I still want to keep you here for a few days—"

"Nah, I'm going home today."

"It's not really recommended, but are you refusing treatment?"

"Yeah, I am. Can't you just come to my house, or I can have another doctor stop by? Either way, I'm taking my ass home."

"Ok, I'll get everything together for you."

He left out, and I tried to pull myself up out of the bed, but Dez had to help me.

"You sure you wanna leave? You can barely move around. You can stay back home until you heal."

"Naw, my girl gon' take care of me. Ain't that right, bae?"

Mel just shook her head and started getting everything together. Ma helped me get dressed in a clean outfit and put my Nike slides on my feet.

A nurse came in with a wheelchair and discharge papers so I could leave.

"You should take it easy the next few days. You have stitches we don't want to rip. Do you have someone to help you at home with baths?"

"Yes the fuck he does, thank you. Damien, sign those damn papers before I have to show my ass."

Melodee snatched the papers from the nurse, and Ma didn't make it any better by laughing at her. I was wheeled down to Melodee's car, and I got in the passenger seat. Dez followed behind us, and we all pulled up to my house at the same time. I wasn't fancy like Dez' ass. I didn't need a big ass gate. All I had was a small metal fence, and I was gon' shoot anybody who walked up.

"You gon' take care of my babies too?"

"Them ain't no damn babies. You need to get rid of them until I leave."

"You crazy as hell, they ain't going no damn where. The best I'll do is keep them in their house."

"What the hell some dogs need they own house for?"

"Same thing you need a house for. Keep talking and I'm gon' go Ochocinco on yo ass."

I had small guest house built on the side of my house where my pitbulls slept. I took care of them like children.

"If you headbutt me, I'mma be the one to shoot yo ass this time."

"Damn, that's how you feel? Wait until I tell my Mama how you treating me."

"You better not snitch." She helped me stand up, and Karter pushed the wheelchair behind me.

I was in pain like a mothafucka, but I had something to fix that in the house. I wasn't about to get drugged on all them meds in the hospital. I had some natural medicine for that.

I chose to sleep in the bedroom on the main floor so I didn't have to walk up and down stairs.

Mama cooked a big ass meal, then her, Dez, and Karter left so I could get some sleep.

Melodee rolled up a fat blunt for us to smoke. This was the type of shit I liked, minus me getting shot the fuck up, but niggas was gon' feel me real soon.

"You feel better now?"

"Hell yeah; shit still hurt a little bit, but I'm good."

"That shit was scary as hell. I'm glad you didn't die, though." She rubbed my thigh, and I grabbed my Sprite from the table.

"Damn, it takes me getting shot to get some affection from you?"

"Shut up, you wanna go lay down for a little bit?"

"Naw, I wanna play 2k for a lil' bit."

"You barely got strength in your left hand and you trying to play the game? How did you even get shot in your hand anyway?"

"Shit, I just remember it was lights in my face, but I saw them niggas walk up and point they heat at me. I guess I thought my ass was gon' stop the shit from hitting me, but I was wrong as hell." I start laughing, and Melodee just looked at me with a stale face.

"That is not funny, Dame, you joke about everything,"

"Fuck you mad for? I'm the one had my damn neck split open. If I wanna laugh at the shit, I'mma laugh."

"I'm going to bed." She got up and walked in the bedroom.

"You just gon' leave me out here by myself? I gotta piss, Melodee, come on. Stop being petty." I was steering the wheelchair with my one good hand, and Mel just sat there watching me.

"Come on and help me, don't be like that. I'm handicapped and you gon' do me like this?"

"Ain't nothing wrong with yo ass."

She wheeled me to the bathroom and helped me stand up to the toilet. She had to hold to my dick while I peed because I had to use my strength to stay standing up.

"That was the most awkward situation I have ever been in."

"Naw, you real for helping me out."

"Lay down and hush. I'm high and ready to go to sleep."

I laid down, and I swear I had the most uncomfortable sleep of my life. My entire body was hurting so bad I was sweating, but had the chills. I think my body went into shock or some shit. Melodee was wiping my head with a cold rag, and she made me take the pain pills I got from the hospital. The shit worked, and I was knocked out twenty minutes after taking them.

"Get up, Dame. You need to take a shower, your clothes are sticking to your body from sweating so much."

I had a shower chair in the bathroom, so I sat in that while I showered. Mel helped wash my hair and back, then helped me get changed into some fresh clothes. I was starting to see Melodee in a new light after this. I saw she was somebody I needed in my life because she was here, and I was definitely at my lowest. For that, she'd be set for life, no matter what happened with us.

Karter

The end of summer was approaching, and I was trying to put together a big Back to School block party for the kids. Along with making sure everyone was prepared to walk in the Bud Billiken Parade, I had my 14 and up class performing at the party as well. Right now, the baby class had just got dismissed, and the older girls were starting to show up.

I went to my office to call Dez, and he answered on the first ring.

"Wassup, baby?"

"Nothing, about to get ready for practice. The girls are so freaking nervous, I don't know what else to do."

"Don't let they little asses dance then."

"Bae, I want everyone to dance. I was thinking about getting them into some local competitions."

"They can't even get it together for they family, you gon' let them go out and embarrass themselves, and you in front of some strangers?"

"I'm about to hang up on you. Trust, I won't be embarrassed because my girls can dance their asses off."

"I'm just playing, baby. I know you the best at what you do and you gone get them together."

"Yeah, whatever. I'm about to go. I don't know how long we're going to here, but I'll text you."

"Aite, I'm over here with bro and 'nem. Melodee said she on her way up there."

"Ok, bye."

I walked out and saw the girls were all on their phones, talking and not stretching like they knew they're supposed to. I was always told I was too easy on them, so it was time I got my Coach D on.

"We got three days until the parade and you all's big performance, and instead of rehearsing LIKE YOU SHOULD BE, I got people on Snapchat, and y'all playing like you got it. So, let's see who really got it, I want y'all to get in position. We're starting from the top, and I want to see you dance full out, and if I feel you're not ready, you're getting cut! We have a lot riding on this. This is going to be the first time that'll we will be introduced to the world. So, let's see if we're getting laughed at or not.

The girls start running around, trying to get in place as I went to the music on my phone. I pressed play on the mix and put my phone down on the floor. All the girls were watching me with wide eyes as I got in position. The music started, and I was dancing along with them. When the song went off, I had them do it again, and I sat with my clipboard. I tried to keep my face stern, but I was smiling seeing my team perform, looking like we'd been doing this for years instead of a few months.

The door opened, and Melodee came in smiling hard looking at the girls.

"Yaaassss, bestie. This is about to lit, I can't wait until Saturday."

"Thanks boo, what you doing up here?"

"Chile, I wasn't about to sit in the house with them, don't let me interrupt."

I walked back in front of the girls and turned the music off.

"That was really good, y'all. We need to work on some of the forms, but it's good so far."

"You should dance with us, Coach Kay. Like you said, this is the first time we're getting introduced, you should do a solo," Jayna, the captain spoke up, and everyone else was cosigning her.

"I'll think about it. Y'all keep practicing, and I'll be watching on the camera." I went to my office, and Melodee came and laid across the couch.

"What's going on, Melly Mel?"

"Nothing, happy to get out the house. I don't know when they're going to open the club again, or if they're going to open it."

"How has Dame been feeling?"

"His crazy ass is fine. Sometimes, he's in pain and we just get high to block out the pain. It works for him, so hey." It had been a few weeks since the shooting, and thankfully, he was healing just fine.

"Is he gon' come out Saturday?"

"Well, I know I'll be there, so if he don't wanna sit at home alone, he'll be there."

"Ok, let me go back in here, you staying?"

"Yeah, I'm 'bout to take a nap, though."

It was after 9 o'clock when I finally let the team out for the night.

"Be here tomorrow at four. DO NOT be late, or you're not dancing. I have new costumes coming for the parade and for your big performance, so make sure I have all sizes before you leave. See you tomorrow."

I opened the front door, and they all rushed outside to their waiting parents. Melodee had already left, and Dez had just pulled to the front of the building to pick me up. I grabbed what I needed out of my office and made sure everything was locked up.

"Wassup, future wife, how was everything?"

"It was good. I'm excited for everything, did you get a DJ for me?"

"Yeah man, I told you I got it. Everything is ready, you gotta relax."

Dez drove us home, and I took a long bath in the Jacuzzi tub. When I was done, Dez was coming in the house with a bag from the Jerk chicken spot that just opened up.

"What you get me?"

"Same thing you always get, a jerk salad."

"Thank you, baby. I know we haven't got a lot of time together these last few weeks, but I appreciate everything you do for me."

"It ain't shit. We both taking care of business, I ain't tripping."

"When are you thinking about opening the club back up?"

"Not anytime soon. I'm changing some shit up, and I'm waiting on Dame." He stuffed his mouth with chicken and was talking with his mouth full. I was looking at him with my lip turned up, and he threw some macaroni at me.

"Come on, I just got out the tub."

"Well, stop looking at me like that, this shit hot."

"If you slow down... ain't nobody gon' take yo food bae

"Shiiiit, you never know with yo ass."

I rolled my eyes and ate my salad while Dez was checking emails and watching SportsCenter as, always.

"I'm going to bed, how long you gon' be?"

"I'm coming right now." He turned the TV off and walked upstairs with me. "You tired, or you tooting that ass up for me?"

"You gotta wait, I'm out of birth control."

"I ain't waiting shit, I'll pull out."

"I don't believe you."

"Good, cuz I'm lying. I'll try to make it quick, though."

He flipped me on my back and kissed me down my body, until he got to my kitty. I only had on a long shirt, so my bottom half was exposed. When I felt his cool breath blowing on my lips, it sent chills through my body. Dez lifted my shirt over my head and positioned himself at my opening. Usually, when he said it's going to be quick, it was a lie, so got ready for an all-night session.

*****

It was the day of the parade, and I was running around trying to make sure everything was perfect. Dez had dropped me off at the dance studio at six this morning, and I had been rehearsing my special performance ever since.

I gave the team the night off to relax last night, but we had a mandatory practice at eight in the morning since the parade started at eleven. It was a quarter to eight, and surprisingly, everyone had arrived already.

"We're going to go over the marching routine first, and while the babies are getting dressed, I'll work with the big girls."

We went through the routine for almost two hours, until the makeup artist I hired showed up

"Hurry up and change, the bus is on the way."

The first uniform we were wearing was a sleeveless, purple and gold, legging-style jumpsuit with gold sequin fringe covering the open midriff. When the bus pulled up, all my dancers piled on, and some of the parents just followed in their cars.

Wya, bae?

Pulling up now

We pulled up to the start of the parade, and I stood up to make my announcement.

"This is the starting point, guys. Remember, we are walking the entire parade. We might get tired, but please keep moving and smiling. We do have a float that the little ones will be on, but I don't want to see any playing. Parents, I love you all and thank you for lending me your kids, but this is your stop. You can walk behind the dancers, but I don't want you all breaking my line. These little smiling faces belong to me now, so get out." Everyone started laughing as the parents got off the bus.

"Ok, grab your pom poms, and make sure you have everything because you won't be coming back to the bus until you get to the finish line. Is everybody ready?"

"Yes."

"I can't tell, that was dry, let me try it again. ARE Y'ALL READY?"

"YESSSSSS!!!"

"That's more like it, let's go."

I led the girls off the bus, and the crowd standing outside start clapping and cheering us on. Melodee was on the float to help the little ones, while Dame was in charge of driving it.

I gave Dez a quick kiss before I went to lead the group. We were being followed by Thornwood High School's marching band since they won Battle of the Bands last year.

By the time we got to the end of parade on 55th and Garfield, the crowd was huge and there were news station crews set up all over. I did a few interviews, where I formally introduced the team as the Divas of Chicago Dance Team and invited everyone out to Brainerd Park, where the Back to School festival was taking place.

As I was walking back to the bus with the girls, I heard someone scream that there was gun before we heard gunshots ring out.

"Run to the bus, girls, hurry up!" I was literally pushing them to get on the bus, and trying to find Melodee, Dez, and Dame in the crowd of people running.

"Karter, get the fuck on the bus!" Dez ran to me, and we got on the bus together.

"Where's Melodee and Dame?"

"In my car, they good, you got everybody?" I looked around the bus and counted heads as the bus driver pulled off quickly.

"Yeah, they're all here. I can't believe people were shooting, knowing all the kids that was there, it's just sad."

"Don't stress on that, baby girl; just keep your eyes on the prize, and that's the big performance later."

He kissed me on the lips, and I did some deep breathing so I could calm down. We made it to Brainerd Park, and I led the girls to an empty room so everyone could change again.

"Parents, once the babies get dressed, they're free to go play, but my big Divas stay back. We need to practice a little more."

When it was time for the big performance, everyone was nervous and shaking.

"Everyone huddle up. Jayna lead us into prayer."

"Ok." She cleared her throat as everyone gathered around and held hands. "Lord, I come to you today asking to erase all of our nerves and self-doubt. Continue to watch over us, and keep us safe as we dance and outside of the studio. Amen."

"Amen."

"Good job. You're all great dancers and will go very far. Shake it off one more time, then line up so we can go."

I led the girls out, and they took the stage to kill it. After my surprise solo, there were a lot of parents that wanted to sign their children up. The Back to School festival went off without a hitch, and I was super happy. In no time, the Divas' name would be ringing bells all over.

Dezmund "Dez"

It had been almost two months since Dame got shot, and I was finally able to track where Malik and his brother, Perry, hung out. They thought shit was sweet because we hadn't made any moves yet, but that wasn't the case at all. Dame wanted to wait until he got some of his strength back in his left arm before he was ready for his revenge.

I pulled up to his house and beeped twice before he came swaggering to my truck.

"Took yo ass long enough."

"Maaann, shut the fuck up. Mel ass been tripping lately. You know she hid all my damn guns?"

I cracked up laughing as I drove away from his house.

Ma guilted us into closing the club, so we decided to open a 24-hour daycare near Karter's dance studio on 95th street. Promise Child Care Academy has been open for two weeks, and we already needed more staff for all the children we were getting.

Once we made sure everything was running smooth at the daycare, we left to handle some other business.

I got to 87th and Carpenter and flipped the block three times looking for Malik and Perry, but these niggas was like Nemo out here. I parked on the side of the liquor store and followed Dame inside.

"Wassup Dame, how you feeling, bro? I heard about what happened."

"I'm good, you seen that nigga, Malik, around here?"

"Shiiiit, earlier; he be in and out, though."

"When you see him, tell him come see me." Dude nodded his head, and we left out the store.

I dropped him off at his house, and went to the studio to check on Karter. The front door was locked, but I had a key so I opened it and locked the door back. She had the music blasting, and she was in the mirror dancing. She was all into what she was doing, and she didn't even notice me standing there until she turned around.

"Oh shit, Dez! You scared the hell outta me."

"My bad, bae. That shit looked good as hell, though."

"Thank you. I was going to teach it to the Divas later on, trying to get them ready for competitions."

"Don't push 'em too hard, baby."

"I'm nooooot. What were you doing, though?"

"Shit, checked on the daycare, then came and saw about my baby. Why you haven't said anything about the wedding, though? Are you even planning it?"

"I mean, yeah, but I've been so busy with the studio. I'm sorry."

Hearing her say that had me heated. It had been a minute, and usually, females be quick with this stuff.

"You ain't trying to marry a nigga."

"Dez, don't be dramatic, I didn't say I ain't wanna marry you."

"You ain't have to say it, you showing me. I'll see you at the crib." I stood up to leave, and Karter rolled her eyes up to the ceiling.

"I can't believe you're really acting like that. I moved out of my Big Mama's house to be with you, and you're questioning me?"

"Yeah, I hear you."

"Get the fuck out! Hurry up, before I say something I can't take back. I swear, you can give a mothafucka the world, and they'll be mad they ain't get the sun too."

"Yo Karter, shut the fuck up, you sound retarded."

"No, you shut the fuck up, Dezmund, and don't worry about picking me up tonight."

"Yup." I walked out the door and had to laugh to myself. Karter's little ass really just tried to turn up on me.

I hopped in the car and headed to Chicago Ridge Mall. I didn't need shit, but I wanted to walk around and clear my head. It was only two in the afternoon, but the mall was semi packed. I grabbed some pizza and sat down in the food court. A cute, dark-skinned female walked past and I can admit, I looked a little longer than I should've.

"Hey, what are you doing here alone?" She came back around and slid into the booth with me.

"I'm just eating."

"You mind if I sit here?"

"You already are." I got a good look at her, and she kind of reminded me a Karter. "What's your name?"

"Jazmyne, but everyone calls me Jazz. What's your name?"

"Dez."

"I've heard a lot about you. Now, I can put a face to the name. It's nice to meet you. Are you single, Dez?"

"Naw, I'm actually engaged."

"Well, does she allow you to have friends?"

"I'm a grown ass man, what you mean allow me to?"

"Well, excuse me. Give me your phone so I can put my number in it." I gave her my phone, and she gave me her number. Females were real bold nowadays; they didn't care about approaching you first no mo.

Dame called me, and I excused myself from the table. "I'll hit you up, Jazz. Wassup, bro?"

"Shit, I'm bored as fuck. Melodee went to go pick Karter up, what the hell you do?"

"I ain't do shit, her ass just spazzed for no reason." I got in the car and pulled off to Dame's house.

"That ain't what it sounded like to me, sis was on go."

"Shut the fuck up and open the door, bitch."

"Nigga, don't bring that negativity in my crib, it's peaceful in here." I hung up on him and got out the car. The door still wasn't unlocked, and I had to knock on the door.

"Nigga, I told yo cripple ass to open the door."

"Fuck you, I was taking a shit."

"You could've kept that to ya self. What you got to eat in here?"

"Shiiiit, Destini dropped a lasagna off that Ma made, it's in the oven now."

"Hell yeah! Why the fuck I don't get no deliveries?"

"I'm her favorite son, that's why." We walked to the kitchen, and I poured a cup of Hennessy from his liquor cabinet.

"Don't tell me you dun ran Karter away already?"

"Naw, she don't wanna be here, so I ain't forcing her. I mean, she ain't even thought about the fucking wedding. That mean she don't wanna get married, right?"

"Nah, she love yo ugly ass. Maybe she just been stressed with the studio and shit."

"Yeah ok." I continued drinking, and I don't remember much after that.

I woke up in a bed that didn't belong me to or anybody I knew, and I was only in my boxers. I heard a toilet flush, and Jazz came out the bathroom wearing some sexy ass lingerie.

Fuck!

I really hope I ain't fuck up like that.

"Hey, I been trying to wake you up, your phone has been blowing up."

I jumped up, threw my pants on that were on the floor, and checked my phone. I had ten missed calls from Karter, and I started feeling worse than I already was.

"Look, I don't know what happened last night or what was said, but like I said before, I'm engaged and I love my girl."

"Ok, you don't have to say all of that. I'm not looking for a relationship, you called me."

She put a robe on and walked out the room. After I made sure I had everything, I followed her out the room and walked right out the front door. I heard her smack her lips, but I didn't give a fuck. I had to go. I saw my car parked all fucked up and had to shake my head, I was gon' have to see why Dame ass let me drive fucked up like that.

I made it home and saw Karter storming to her, car pissed off. She looked at me, and I saw was hurt in her eyes.

"Where you going? And why is all yo clothes and shit in the car? Karter, stop fucking playing with me, where you going?"

"I'm going home. I waited here all night worried, thinking something happened to you, and you was just with the next bitch."

"What you talking about, bae?"

"The bitch answered your phone, Dezmund."

She got in her car and sped out the gate. I just stood there with my hands on top of my head. I wished I could tell Karter nothing happened, but I honestly didn't know if it did or not.

Damn, I fucked up.

Karter

I was doing 60 all the way home, and I didn't care if I got pulled over or not. I couldn't believe Dez cheated on me after one stupid fight. I pulled up to my house and let out a sigh of relief because Mel's car wasn't outside. I didn't feel like playing 21 questions; I wanted to be alone. Dez had called me about five times, and I ignored every last one of them. Once I was done dragging my bags into the house, I looked through the fridge to see if there was something to eat. Melodee hadn't been here in weeks and neither had I, unless I was checking the mail. Everything in the fridge was out dated, so I went to change out of my pajamas so I could go to the store. I didn't feel like getting cute, so I threw on some leggings and a tank top.

I went to the Target on 119th and Marshfield because I needed to do a little retail therapy too. I walked around every department, buying stuff for home and the dance studio. I ended up spending over eight hundred dollars on stuff I didn't really need, and didn't even buy my groceries. Once I stuffed my trunk and backseat, I headed to the studio to drop everything off, and to blow off some steam.

Just as I was looking for the perfect song, Melodee called me.

"Hey Mel, I'm at the studio, wassup?"

"I don't know what's going on, but Dez showed up like an hour ago and was going nuts. Him and Dame fought and everything. He kept screaming, talking about you wasn't coming back. I was tryna find out where the hell you went."

"I don't really wanna talk about it, but I moved back into the house."

"I agreed to work at the daycare overnight, but I'll be there in the morning. Anyway, your birthday is coming up, what are we doing?"

"I'm not in the birthday mood, but whatever you plan, I'll be there."

"I was about to say, don't let no nigga ruin yo birthday. You better boss up on him. How about we do a black and gold themed party at the club."

"The club is closed, Mel."

"And I got the keys, so that bitch gon' open that night. Oohhh yeessss, it'll be fun, I'll handle it from here. How 'bout you work on a sexy ass dance for us too? I'll dust off my dancing shoes for you, boo."

"Aite, I'll do that now, I already got the perfect song."

"Alright, Kay bay."

We hung up, and I turned on "When We" by Tank. I'd been seeing so many videos with different choreography, so I wanted to kill it next.

It was dark by the time I decided to go home, and I was beyond tired. As soon as I opened the studio door to leave, Dez was standing there with his eyes low and red.

"So, you really just gon' leave me?" The kush on his breath was so strong, I got a contact high from him being so close to me.

"Dezmund, clearly you're not ready for this relationship, so I'm helping you out."

He pushed me back into the studio, and I almost tripped over the bags I brought in earlier.

"I'm ready to go home now, can you go?"

"Can you just let me explain what happened before you just walk away from this?"

"You got five minutes, I'm tired."

"Karter, I promise I don't remember what happened last night."

"Where were you?"

He started scratching his head, and I just knew the next thing that came out his mouth was going to be a lie.

"Aite look, after we had our little argument and shit, I went to the mall and this shorty approached me, and gave me her number.

"Sooo, you fucked her?"

"Man, listen! I went to Dame's crib, and we was drinking and shit. I don't know how the fuck I ended up at her crib, but I was there when I woke up."

"Is that it?"

"Pretty much, yeah. Are we ok now?"

I started laughing like he told the funniest joke in the world. "No, we're not ok now! You fucked this random bitch you met AT THE MALL, and you think I'm going to just say forget it?"

"I was fucking drunk, Karter!"

"And, you should've brought yo drunk ass home to me instead of the next bitch. Sorry, not sorry. Now, can I leave?"

We left out, and I locked the door and set the alarm. Dez sped off as soon as I reached my car, and I just shook my head. Since I didn't get to eat, I grabbed a chicken salad from Wendy's and went home.

The next morning, I awakened to Melodee singing loudly in the kitchen.

"Karter Dream! Wake up, heffa!"

I groaned and rolled out the bed.

"What the hell? Why are all these flowers in here?"

"Why you think?"

I rolled my eyes and sat down on a stool. "Well, he can keep this shit."

"Girl, what did he do, because ain't nobody telling me shit?"

"He cheated on me with a girl he met in the mall."

"He actually told you?"

"He said he got drunk and woke up in her bed. What else could've happened? He should've drove the hell home; instead, he went there."

"I meeeaannn, you don't know if he cheated. I say we go find the bitch and ask her."

"No, thank you."

"Y'all are so cute together, in an irritating way. I'm kinda sad about this."

"Yeah, me too. I think I just suck at relationships."

"You and me both. I'm shocked I haven't left Dame's ass yet."

"Girl, you ain't fooling me. I know you're in love, you'll be married before me."

Melodee tried to hide her smile, and I thought it was cute she was acting like a schoolgirl. "I wouldn't say I'll marry his ass, Dame is—I don't know what Dame is, but I don't think I can deal with his crazy ass for the rest of my life."

"Yeah, I feel you."

"I did tell him that we're opening the club for your birthday and he agreed, not like he had a choice. But, you know Dez is going to be there, right?"

"Good, I want him to be."

"That's what I'm talking about. Now, I'm going to bed, wake me up before you leave."

I went back to lay down too; she acted like she wasn't the one who woke me up.

****

The days leading up to my birthday party had been crazy. Dez had been popping up on me wherever I went, which was only to the studio and back home. Yesterday, a girl who told me her name was Jazz showed up at the studio to explain to me that she didn't do anything with Dez. I heard her out, and still wanted to knock her head off. When she told me how he told her he was engaged and she still tried to shoot her shot, it took everything in me not to reach out and touch her. But, enough of that. It was my 27th birthday, and I was ready to forget about all my problems.

Melodee had been treating me like royalty today; she got my nails and feet done, and I was currently sitting in the shop getting some bundles installed, courtesy of

Melodee. I chose some dark brown, 26-inch Brazilian virgin hair, and I was feeling like 'new hair who this?'

"Bestie, you know you fine, I can't wait to see you in your outfit."

"Thanks, boo. I can't wait to get there."

Melodee paid, and we got in her car to go home. I put my bonnet on and hopped in the shower before I got dressed. I was wearing a royal blue, halter bandage dress that stopped at the middle of my thigh, and my gold Giuseppe Zanotti sandals.

When I was grabbing my purse, I noticed a set of car keys that didn't belong to me sitting on my dresser. I grabbed them and walked out of my room.

"Mel! Whose keys are—"

Dez was sitting on the couch, looking like the king he was. He had on a navy blue, Armani Collezioni, 'G-Line' style suit and some matching blue loafers. His gold watch was shining bright, along with the gold grill in his mouth.

"Happy birthday, Karter."

"Thank you, Dezmund. Are these your keys?"

"Nah, they're yours, go outside."

I walked to the window and pulled the drapes back. There was a matte blue Mercedes G Wagon parked in the middle of the street, and my mouth was hanging open.

"What the hell did I tell you about buying me shit like this? Don't think this makes up for what you did."

"Why can't you just say thank you like a regular person?"

"Because, I'm not a regular, mothafucka, but thank you." I walked out the house and to the truck to examine it. The inside was leather, and the trunk could fit so many shopping bags.

"You know, yo attitude has been fucked up lately, wassup with you?"

"Besides the fact that you cheated, I mean, I've been good. I don't know what you're talking about." I got out the truck so I could lock the house up, and Dez grabbed my hand and got on one knee.

"Dezmund, get up, you're going to get dirty."

"I don't give a fuck about that. Can we move past this, please? I still want you to be my wife, Karter, do you still want to marry me?" He took my ring out his pocket, and I couldn't stop the smile that spread across my face.

"Yes, but I swear, if you even think about another bitch, I'll kill you."

"Damn bae, you sexy as hell when you get crazy on me."

"Shut up, come on. You're driving." I locked up and got in the passenger side of my new truck.

"I love this, and it rides so smooth."

"I thought you'd like it, and I ain't know what else to get you for yo birthday. Plus, I was tired of seeing you stuff that damn car with bags, you shop too damn much."

"Shut up, it's always stuff that's needed, though." He didn't know about the stuff I had delivered to my house on the regular. I had a shopping habit, and he didn't make it any better. We pulled up to the club, and it was decorated beautifully. We parked at the front door, and Dez walked around to open the door for me. There was a royal blue carpet that led all the way to the door. Melodee really went extra with it. A photographer came out, and I took some pictures with Dez, and some alone.

"Happy Birthday!"

The club was packed, and I'm pretty sure I didn't know any of the people there.

"Bestie, you so fiiinne. I see you wearing that ring again, Team Karter and Dez."

"You so irra, who are all these damn people?"

"Girl, I put a flyer on Facebook. You know niggas showing up for liquor, food, and music. Here, Queen, put your crown on." She handed me a gold crown that was covered in diamonds.

"Girl, you gon' get me robbed."

"Dez will kill them before they could get away, you good."

She led me to my section, and I was ready to put on my performance. There was a small stage put on the dance floor, and this is perfect. Dez might be a little mad when he saw what I was gonna do, but that was my intention when I made it.

"You nervous?" Dez scooted into the booth where I was and kissed me on my lips.

"No, I'm ready to do it now."

"Go change then."

He stood up and led me to his office, where my bag was.

"Hurry up."

As soon as the door closed, I was taking my dress off and putting on the shorts and halter top I had in my bag. I put on my peep toes booties and texted Melodee to have the lights dimmed low. I maneuvered through the crowd, walked onto the stage, and got in my stance.

When we, fuck

When we, fuck

Tank's song "When We" started to play through the speakers, and I did a leg hold. I literally held my leg in the air for three seconds before Dez was snatching me off stage. The entire club was laughing at me as Dez carried me over his shoulder, and up the stairs to his office. He locked the door and pulled a chair out for him to sit in.

"You got me fucked up if you thought I was letting you do that in front of all them niggas. Turn that music on, and show me what you was finna do."

I plugged my phone up to his speakers and started the song. By the time I got done dancing, Dez was biting his lip and coming out of his suit.

"What you doing, Dez?"

"I'm 'bout to do you, now get on that desk."

I took my clothes off and hopped on his cold desk. Dez approached me and went right to my neck. He knew that drove me crazy, and I was soaking his desk in seconds. I let out a low moan, and Dez entered me slowly.

"Mmmm, this shit still tight, bae. Don't ever call yourself leaving me again. You hear me, Karter?"

"Yesssss, I hear you, Dez." He lifted me up and pinned me against the wall. I'm pretty sure everybody heard us over the music, but I didn't care.

When we were done, we took a quick shower in his private bathroom, and I got dressed again. This time, I put on a short black dress with gold accessories. Dez was looking at me funny, and I started feeling self-conscious. I knew I had gained like five pounds, and I thought his rude ass was about to say something about it.

"You got us looking like some G's with this blue and black. Why you ain't tell me you was changing, bro? I think I got a black suit in my closet, hold on."

"Bye Dezmund, I'll see you when you done."

"Petty ass."

I walked back down to the main floor, and Melodee was waiting with a tray full of shots.

"Girl, why is that brown, what the fuck?"

"It's Hennessy biiiittcch, turn up! It's your 27th birthday, and Hennything's possible!" I sat back in my original seat and said a quick prayer before I took the ten shots Melodee had lined up in front of me.

"You trying to get sis fucked up. Happy birthday, Karter."

"Thank you, Dame."

Dez came in the section with his own personal bottle of Dusse', and he was drinking it straight from the top.

"Y'all about to make me some nieces and nephews tonight drinking that shit."

I poured myself a cup of Hennessy and was sipping and dancing in my seat.

Pnb Rocks' single "Hanging Up My Jersey" came on, and Dez pulled me in his lap as he rapped along with the song in my ear.

"So shawty where you at 'cause I'm around? I'm hanging up my jersey for yooouu."

"Bae, you cannot sing."

"Shut up, girl."

I laughed as he finished singing in my ear. "Right now, I'm right down. My side of town, I'm high as hell, you fly as hell. You hold me down, I'mma hold you down too."

I was dancing in his lap as I finished drinking my Hennessy. I was glad I could get back into my happy place, with my king.

Dezmund "Dez"

Karter's drunk ass was asleep sitting in my lap, and it was only one in the morning. I had the DJ call last call so we could shut this shit down. By two o'clock, I was letting the DJ out and carrying Karter to the car.

"Bro, look, this nigga bold as hell."

I looked to where Dame was looking and saw Malik and his brother standing across the street from us. I put Karter in the car, and Melodee got in the backseat. I took my jacket off and covered Karter in it, then walked across the street with Dame.

"I heard y'all was looking for me." I didn't respond to Malik as I punch him in the jaw so hard I heard it crack.

Dame punched Perry, and he hit the ground right next to his brother. I could've easily shot this nigga for shooting my brother, but I wanted them to remember this ass whooping before I killed 'em.

"Dame, that's enough! Dez, stop y'all, please! Karter, wake up!" Melodee got out the car screaming, and Dame instantly stood up and went to check on her.

"What's wrong, bae? Get back in the car."

"No, get Dez now before he kills him!"

I stood up and wiped the blood off my hands with Malik's shirt. I walked past Melodee and Dame and got in truck with Karter.

Pick up in front of the spot NOW

I sent a text out to a number I didn't think I'd have to use again. They didn't reply, but they showed me they read it, so I know they were on the way to clean up.

I drove home, and Karter woke up when I cut the truck off.

"Baby, what happened?"

"Nothing, come on.

She could barely walk, and I had to help her walk up the stairs to the bedroom.

"You got blood all over your suit— who's bleeding Dezmund? Where is Melodee and Dame?"

"Shut up, Karter, they at home now probably."

"You're lucky my head is spinning, I'll start this conversation over in the morning."

"Yeah, ok."

I went to go take a shower, and I scrubbed every inch of my body and hair four times before I got out the tub and joined Karter in the bed. She was stretched across the bed, so I moved her over so I could lay behind her.

The next morning, I woke up and made Karter some coffee and brought her saltine crackers. I knew she was going to be throwing up all morning because she always did that when she was drinking.

"Hello?"

"Hey, Mr. Wright, there's someone here that said she wanted to apply for the overnight position."

"Ok, I'll be there in a minute. Give her a tour of the facility and an application.

"Ok."

I went to my closet to find something to wear, and Karter sat up in bed. "Where you going?"

"To the daycare, somebody wants the overnight position, so I'mma go interview her."

"Ok, bring me an Italian beef dipped with extra peppers."

"Yo ass gon' be sick."

"It'll be worth it."

I grabbed some jeans, a white shirt, and a tan blazer.

"You looking too good, go change."

"Stop tripping and lay back down, I'll be right back."

I gave her a kiss on the forehead and drove my Jeep to the daycare.

When I walked in the door and saw Jazz sitting in my office, everything told me to walk back out.

"This is your place?"

"So, you didn't know?"

"No, I didn't. I just need a job. I have my degree." Her ass was lying; I knew she was.

"Ok, so have you actually worked in a daycare before? This ain't about babysitting, the kids need to learn while they're having fun."

"Dez, I take my job very serious."

"It's Mr. Wright, but I hope you do. There are cameras everywhere. I'll have Robin give you all the paperwork you need filled out, and she'll get you a key. When can you start?"

"Tonight, if you need me to."

"Ok, be back at 10 on the dot. Welcome to the team." I held my hand out, and she rolled her eyes before she shook it. I left right back out the door and got in the car. I drove to Portillos to get Karter's food, and I went right back home.

"Oohhh, it smells so good."

"I gotta tell you something."

"What the hell happened that fast?"

"Jazz, she work at the daycare now."

"Are you fucking serious, Dezmund? After everything we just went through, you go and hire her?"

"We need the help, ma. Don't start spazzing on me."

"Whatever."

"Karter, don't be like that. Karter? You just gon' ignore me? I swear, you be petty as hell." She kept ignoring me, and she sat eating her food like I wasn't talking to her.

I didn't understand what she wanted me to do. Ain't like she was going to work there, and I sure as hell wasn't doing it. I took my clothes off and laid back down. If Karter wasn't gon' talk to me, I was taking my ass to sleep.

"Son you just gon' lay down, you just don't give a fuck, huh?"

"Karter, what the fuck are you talking about?"

"Forget it. If you don't care, I don't care either." She stomped out the room, and I had to count to twenty before I got up to follow her.

"Bae, are you on yo period?"

"No, why the hell would you ask me that?"

"Shit, I'm tryna make sense of this crazy ass shit you doing."

"Every time I don't agree with you about something, you say I'm acting crazy."

I just sat down and stared at her. I didn't know what she wanted me to say at this point, but I wasn't about to be arguing with her all day.

"What you want me to do, you want me fire her?"

"No, then you gon' blame me for why you understaffed."

"I just want to make you happy, Karter. Tell me what to do, and I'll do it."

"Nothing. It's fine, Dez. Just don't fuck up."

"I'm not, bae. Now, come rub my back while I bust Dame's ass in 2k."

****

So far, the decision to hire Jazz had been a big ass mistake. She called me all times of night, talking about she heard something outside. I ain't have a problem making sure the kids were safe, but she was over doing it.

"Dez, I swear the next time that girl calls you at two in the morning again, I'm gon' beat her ass."

"Not in front of the kids, you not."

"I'm sure them kids seen worse shit than somebody getting beat up. I wouldn't do that, though. I don't even like violence, but people like to push buttons, and that bitch trying to be funny."

"How, Karter Dream?"

"Don't do that, Dezmund Anthony."

"Come on, bae. Let's plan the wedding, where the iPad at?"

"What you mean THE iPad? You mean MY iPad?"

"You selfish as hell."

We laid across the couch all day planning our big day, and we had almost everything together, except what we were wearing.

"Do you think Ma is going to fly?"

"Yeah, she might drink a little bit before the flight, but she'll be alright."

"I'm going back to sleep. Wake me up when you figure out what's for dinner."

Karter went upstairs to lay down, and I checked my emails that had been piling up all morning. People had been trying to get me to open the club back up, but I didn't know. Even though we got Malik taken care of, I didn't know if I wanted to be so reachable. We'd see how that went.

Karter

I was lying in bed with my Kindle, finally finishing *Us Before Anything 2* by Ms. Brii, and I got a Facetime from Dez. He was out at the daycare, and I was at home eating Oreos.

"Hey bae, what you doing?"

"Shit, about to head out in a minute."

I looked at the time, and it was past midnight. "Where you going?"

"I'm about to run and grab some Subway right quick."

"You better not be getting that bitch some food."

"Come on, baby, we talked about this."

"Fine Dezmund."

"You in the bed?" He was looking around like he could really see what's going on in my background.

"Nah, I'm at a friend's house, he went to get us some drinks."

Beep

I sat with my mouth hanging open— this nigga really hung up on me. I called back three times before he finally answered.

"What the hell, Dezmund, why hang up on me— are you in the car?"

"Hell yeah! I'm on my way back, you got me fucked up."

I fell out laughing, holding my stomach as he mugged me through the camera.

"You crazy as hell. I'm at home Dez, look."

I got up to turn the lights on and showed him the room before I turned the camera back around and shut the lights off.

"Karter, stop doing dumb shit, man."

"It was a joke. What friends do I have besides Melodee?"

"You suck at telling jokes, ma. Stick to dancing and shit. How long you gon' be up?"

"For a minute, I'm trying to finish this book or I'm not gon' able to sleep."

"I might be back late tonight. I love you, I gotta go."

"I love you too." I hung up and laid back with my tablet, reading.

I don't know when Dez got in, I didn't even hear the alarm chime. I was too busy sitting with my mouth wide, staring at my tablet screen.

"Bugs, why you over there looking stupid?" He walked to the dresser and put his gun, keys and phone down.

"I'm worried about Kori; if something happened to her, I know Lah gon' lose his shit if she hurt."

"Who is that?"

"From the book, Dez!" I slammed my tablet down and folded my arms across my chest.

"What the hell you pouting for?"

"Because, I'm mad I have to wait on part three. Do you think she's done writing it? Can we go to Portland?"

"For what?" He pulled a pair of American Eagle boxer briefs out and threw them on the bed.

"I need to talk to her, bae. I can't just let it go without knowing what happened."

He stopped his stride to the bathroom and looked at me. "I'm not about to stalk that girl because you a book junkie. Bring yo ass on in the shower, and don't say shit else about a damn book."

I followed behind him, still pouting as he turned the shower on.

I stripped out of my clothes and stepped into the shower before him to adjust the water. People liked to say women took hot showers, but no. Dez acted like he was trying to burn the black off me when we showered together.

He stepped in behind me and started kissing on my neck as he palmed my small breast.

"Bae?"

"Hmmm?"

I turned facing him and he brought his lips to mine, kissing me deeply.

"If we were on the phone and I screamed after a loud crashing noise... what would you think happened?"

"Yo, you serious right now? Get out my shower, bro."

Ok ok, I'm sorry, come on." I tried to kiss him, but he muffed me back.

"Get out, I'm dead serious."

"Whatever, don't come in here tryna get no side action either, punk." I stomped in the room with my robe on and grabbed my tablet so I could go post on Brii's group page. #WhatHappenedToKori!

Dez walked out the bathroom with his towel wrapped around his waist, and I watched his every move as he dropped his towel and put his clothes on.

"I see you watching me; if you wasn't so busy worried about a book, you would've got some of this. Now, you ain't getting shit."

"Dez, stop playing with me, I'll take it."

"Yo ass gon' go to jail. That's rape, bruh." He got under the covers, and I turned my butt toward him so I could get comfortable. I felt his member jump and hit me, and I smacked my lips.

"You better move, Dezmund, I wasn't playing with you." He reached his arm around me and stuck his finger in my panties. When I was starting to get into it, he took his hand back and turned over.

"You not playing fair, you better finish what you started."

"Nah, I'm tired."

I climbed on him and made him lay on his back. I took his thick, hard member in my hand and eased down on him. I was moving my hips to a song in my head, and Dez grabbed my hips to move me to his rhythm.

"You trying to show out, huh?"

I laughed as he flipped me over and put my legs on his shoulders. By the time he got done with me, my legs were numb and I knew if I tried to walk, I was going straight to the floor. Dez started snoring, and it scared the shit out of me. It sounded like a grizzly bear was in our room.

His phone vibrated on the dresser, so I got up to answer it. It was the daycare number, and I rolled my eyes.

"Hello?"

"Um hey, this is Jazz. I was trying to reach Dez, I mean Mr. Wright." This girl was testing me. I kept telling Dez she wanted me to snatch her up, and he always claimed I was acting like a bully.

"He's asleep, what is it that you need?"

"Oh, I don't think you're going to be able to help me. I'll try again later, thanks."

She hung up, and I threw Dez's phone down on the dresser. He jumped up out his sleep and reached for his gun he kept next to him.

"If you gon' shoot somebody, it's gon' be that Jazz bitch. You need to hire somebody else and fire that hoe."

"Man, what the fuck happened now? This shit irritating as hell."

"You're absolutely right. It's irritating for a bitch who want my "man" to constantly try me, and you're not doing shit about it. Do you want me to leave so y'all can finish whatever it is y'all started?"

"I swear, you gon' make me shake the snot out yo ass. Ain't nobody thinking about that bitch."

"Well, fire that bitch."

"Aite, well who gon' cover tonight?"

"I don't give a damn. You better get yo sleeping bag and sit the hell in the with them."

"You off them drugs if you think I'm doing that shit."

"Ok, do what you want to do then." I walked to the bathroom and locked the door. I had to pee for the hundredth time, and I wanted some space away from Dez's ass. I hated how he was always making excuses for the next muhfucka when I was the one that was supposed to be his future wife.

"Come out the bathroom, Karter, yo ass can't hide in there forever."

"Shut up."

"Take that pregnancy test that's under the sink while you in there."

I sat on the toilet, frozen in place as I tried to think about when the last time was that I had my period. I grabbed the Clearblue pregnancy test from under sink and ran the faucet so I could pee again.

I followed the directions in the box and waited for the results to pop up. Dez picked the lock and walked into the bathroom. He looked at the test and squinted his eyes.

"You have to wait two minutes, relax."

"Nah baby, that say pregnant already." I pushed him out the way, and sure enough, both of the tests said, 'pregnant 3+'.

"Damn, don't look so excited."

"It's not that, bae. It's just I wasn't really ready for babies. I told you that before, but it's done now."

"Damn right, it's done now."

I couldn't believe I was having a baby. I had my own little plan on how I wanted to do things. I just hoped I didn't blow up and couldn't lose the weight.

I laid down with a million thoughts running through my head.

What am I going to do with a baby?

Melodee

I was at the daycare, making sure all the paperwork was being correctly when this new Karter wannabe came prancing in my office.

"Hey, I'm Jazz, we haven't had a chance to meet."

"That's because I don't care to meet you."

"Oh, you must be one of her friends."

"Aw yeah bitch, you got the right one." I stood up and was walking around my desk when Dame came into my office.

"Bae, sit down. I know that face. Jazz, do you need help with something?"

"No, thank you, I'll just go check on the babies. Nice to meet you."

"Mmmhhmmm." I sat back in my seat, and Dame closed my door and start laughing.

"Melodee, was you gon' beat the girl ass in the daycare?"

"I forgot where I was for a second. Woooo saaaaa. Ok, I'm good."

"Yo ass crazy."

"Naw, that bitch is bold, talking about *aawww, you one of HER friends*. She wasn't about to play with my best friend like that. Karter gon' end up snapping and whooping her ass, and I'mma be right there cheering her on."

"Karter ain't gon' do nothing, you know bro dun knocked her up?"

"Hell yeah, that's funny as hell."

"You next."

"Nigga, you thought. I ain't next for shit."

"Daaammn, you act like having my baby is a big problem."

"Shit, it is. You seen your big ass head? Tuh! I ain't pushing that out of me. I feel sorry for po' lil' Karter. You laughing, and I'm dead serious."

"You funny as hell, though. Don't be coming at my future kids like that. Or my nieces and nephews."

"Shut up, and grab that bag so we can go. I'm hungry bae."

"Now I'm bae cuz yo fat ass hungry?"

"Don't make me give you Jazz's ass whooping." I put my blazer on and walked out the door, hand in hand with Dame.

I almost whooped that Jazz hoe ass!

Omg! Lol I hope no kids or parents were around

Naw, this heffa came to my office, then gon' say aw you one of HER friends

Bitch...

Exactly!

"Damn, you just gon' text the whole car ride? You ain't tell me what you want to eat."

"Go to Smashburger." I put my phone up and turned the music up.

We made it to the restaurant and picked a booth in the corner.

"Welcome to Smashburger, are you ready to place your order?"

"Yeah, I am. I want a bacon avocado club with jalapeno peppers and onions, an order of smash fries, and an Oreo peanut butter malt."

"How do you want your burger cooked?"

"Well done, please."

"And for you, sir?"

"I want the Windy city burger, sweet potato smash fries, and an ice water."

"Ok, I'll be right back with your drinks."

"People really think you somebody, huh?"

"What you talking about?"

"The way people look at you when you walk in the room."

"I had to earn that shit, bae. Yo man a legend out here."

Our drinks were brought out, and we made small talk until our food came. I was happy that me and Dame were finally at a place where we could get along. It took us long enough, but we were getting it right.

"Dame, we need to open the club back up. I love the kids, but I need some turnup in my life."

"Well, put some shit together and we'll see how it go. That club shit is expensive, Mel. We ain't made no profit yet."

"Well, you not gon' do it with the door closed."

"Aite, show me what you can do by Saturday, and I'll talk to Dez."

He paid the bill, and we left out to go to the show. I don't know what had him in such a good mood, but I was gon' take full advantage and do some online shopping.

***

The next day, I was up posting flyers all over Facebook, Instagram, and Twitter. Dame wanted to play, and I think I was following all of Illinois on social media. I knew he saw how packed I got it for Karter's birthday.

"Can you go to the daycare for a couple hours?"

"What the hell? Who called off? Bitches about to be unemployed."

"Just go sit yo ass in the office and handle the phones."

"Ok, I hope won't have to slap nobody in there, Damien."

"Chill out with that. Just stay in the office, unless they really need you."

I got up and changed into some blue jeans and a crop tee. I didn't feel like dressing up; they were getting chill Melodee today.

I got to the daycare and poked my head in every class so that they know I was here before I went to hide in my office. I turned the TV on and sent out emails to the staff we had on hold for the club. Now, all I had to take care of was security — then, it's a lituation.

Karter

It had been a few days since I found out I was pregnant, and I was sitting in the doctor's office waiting on Dez to get here. He had got called to the daycare, AS ALWAYS, because Jazz couldn't handle something else. I felt like she needed to be relieved of her duties if she couldn't get it together.

"Ms. Martin, we can't wait any longer, she's ready for you."

"Ok, I'm sorry about this. I'm ready."

Where the fuck are you?!?

I texted Dez after I got my vitals done because he still wasn't here.

Pulling up bae

"Hey, Karter. What brings you in today?"

"I took a positive pregnancy test at home, so I wanted to just confirm it."

She looked down at the chart and wrote something down. "Well, from the urine sample, it did come back positive, so lay back and we can get a look."

She turned the lights down, and Dez came rushing in the room. I rolled my eyes at him so hard, I think they stuck back there an extra second. "Sorry I'm late."

I didn't acknowledge him as I laid back and let the doctor do the ultrasound. She didn't have the screen toward me, but I was reading her face and it had me scared.

"Is something wrong?" She gave me a small smile, and turned the monitor toward us.

"This is the baby, you looked to be about seven weeks."

"Looked?"

"Yes, unfortunately, I didn't find a heartbeat." I didn't hear anything else she said as I laid on the table, trying to fight my tears. I had just got excited about having a baby, and now it was gone.

"Bugs, it's gon' be ok." Dez wiped my cheek, and I didn't even realize I was crying.

"I'm really sorry, Karter, I'll give you a minute." The doctor left out the door, and I let all my tears out as Dez rubbed my back.

"We can try again, baby."

I rolled my eyes at him and got myself together. The doctor came back in, and she had a stack of papers and some medicine.

"Ok, I'm giving you Misoprostol. This will dissolve in your mouth and help your body move along with the process. I also have some painkillers for you. This will be extremely painful, I'm not going to lie to you."

"Thank you." I stood up with my stuff cradled in my arm, and the doctor gave me a big hug.

"I'll say an extra prayer for you tonight, sweetie."

"I appreciate it." I walked out the door in a hurry and tried to just jump in the truck and leave, but Dez snatched the driver's door open so fast, I had to look at him sideways.

"Why you snatching on my damn door like that?"

"Why the fuck you just gon' leave and not say shit?"

"I was going to see you at home, what is there to say?"

"Aite, I love you, baby."

"Uh huh, love you too."

I closed and locked my door before he could say anything else. I was feeling so many emotions, I couldn't tell if I was mad or sad. I drove home in silence. I didn't have music playing; all I heard was the sound of traffic. Dez followed me all the way to the house, and was hopping out the car fast as hell to open my door.

"You mad at me?"

"Dez, really? I'm about to push our dead baby out in the toilet, and you want know if I'm mad at you?"

"Don't start lashing out at me, bae. I'm hurt about this shit too."

I felt myself about to cry again, so I walked in the house so I could go take a long, hot bath. Dez got my water ready and threw one of my favorite bath bombs into the water. He sat on the toilet the entire time, but he didn't say a word. He sat there, staring at the wall in front of him. I don't even think he blinked.

When I was done, he helped me out and rubbed my body down with my moisturizer.

I got the pills and put two in each cheek, like I was told. When it was all dissolved, I laid down and turned the TV on the Hallmark channel.

"You want something from downstairs, bae?"

"Some water and a cup of ice." It was only 11:30 in the morning, and I don't know what to expect, but she prescribed me hydrocodone, so I could only imagine.

Two hours after I took the pills, I was feeling like I was having the worst period cramps of my life. I was balled up in the middle of the bed, crying while Dez stood his yellow ass in the corner like he was scared to come close.

"Go get me my heating pad, please."

"It's here already, or I gotta leave and get it

"It's under the damn sink, Dezmund!"

I felt like I was dying and he wasn't helping me at all.

"Here, bae."

"Call Melodee, please. Just please go get her."

My stomach was hurting so bad, I couldn't even think straight. I took a pain pill and laid down with the heating pad on my stomach. I was drifting off to sleep when I heard Melodee's voice.

"Karter? I'm so sorry, baby, how you feeling?"

"This shit hurts so bad. If this is what childbirth feels like, I'm never having babies."

Melodee slid into bed with me and got comfortable. She stayed with me, rubbing my back as I went through every cramp, and every trip to the bathroom to change my pad. Melodee left to handle something at the club, and it was just me and Dez sitting in the room.

"You need something, bae?"

"No, I'm good. I just gotta go to the bathroom again." When I went to the bathroom this time, I saw a big blood clot, and I knew that was it. The pain I was feeling had slowly subsided, and I couldn't bring myself to flush the toilet.

"Come on, baby. You need to rest. It's gon' be ok, baby, I promise." Usually, when Dez said that to me, I believed him. But now, I didn't even think he believed himself.

***

After I lost the baby, I kept the studio closed for about two weeks. I was finally feeling better, and was tired of sitting in the house being depressed. To make matters worse, Dez was staying out later and later. At first, he wouldn't leave my side; now, he acted like he couldn't be in the house for more than an hour. I sent out a mass text to the Divas, telling them we were resuming practice this morning, and everyone as excited. When Dez left at seven this morning, I got up and got dressed too.

I entered the girls into a competition that was next week, and there was a captain's solo portion, and I knew Jayna was going to have a fit.

I made it to the studio and got busy cleaning the mirrors, so everyone could see themselves perfectly.

"Hey, Coach Kay, we missed you." All the girls started piling in at the same time.

"I missed y'all too, Jayna. Everybody, line up and stretch. We have a big day ahead of us. Exactly seven days from today, we will be in Wisconsin for competition. We have creative, a captain solo, and stand battle. Can you all handle all three?"

"YESSSS!"

"Good, let's get to work. We're starting on the creative portion. Now, with this, we're using the babies too; they'll be your introduction. Since we're so close to Halloween, that is the theme we're using."

It was after six in the evening by the time I dismissed the girls, and they were all dragging their feet out the door.

"Tomorrow, meet me here at noon. We'll go over the stands more. Since this will be our first time competing, I want you all here every day after school by 5 p.m. Any questions?"

"What about homework?"

"You get out of school at 2:30; you should be able to do homework in three hours. If it's too much for you, let me know and you can sit this one out. I'm not going to baby you. If this is what you want, you're going to work hard for it. Now, if there's no more questions, I'll see you tomorrow."

I stayed behind and worked on some more choreography.

Boom

Boom

Boom

There was banging at the front door, and I peeked out the window to see who it was. Melodee was standing there with her hands on her hips.

"Where the hell have you been?"

"I've been here all morning, Mel."

"We been looking for you; you're not answering the phone. Are you even supposed to be doing all of this so soon?"

"It's either this, or sit in the house depressed all day alone. And, I don't even know where I put my phone when I got here."

"How are you feeling?"

"I don't know, honestly, but I'll be ok."

"Don't shut down on me again, bestie. You know I'm here for you."

"Yeah, but that's it, all I have is you. Dezmund acts like he don't care; we barely even said two words to each other in two weeks. It's like when I lost the baby, I lost him too."

"Awww baby, I'm sorry. Dame did tell me that Dez had been drinking more. Maybe he's trying to deal with it like you are. You two need to talk. You're supposed to be getting married, don't let something that was out of both of your control tear you apart."

I listened to everything Melodee was saying, and just nodded my head. She helped me close up and I drove home, actually hoping Dez wasn't there. But, just my luck, he was pulling up at the same time I was.

"Where you been?"

"At practice, it's nice to see you too." I walked into the house, and went to the kitchen to find something to eat, while Dez grabbed a bottle of liquor and set in front of the TV.

"Karter, come talk to me."

"Wassup?"

"You not the only one that lost something. You know that, right? We're walking around here like strangers and shit, and I ain't feeling it. what's going on with you?"

"It's not me; you're the one who leaves the house at all times of night. You leave early, come back late — you couldn't even be on time to my freaking appointment."

"I was working, bro!"

"That bitch calls you and you go running like a fucking lap dog. But, you couldn't even be there on time to check on a baby you claim you wanted, and it's fucked up. I can't do this anymore, Dezmund, I can't lose anything else."

I tried to walk away, but he grabbed my arm and pulled me into a tight hug. I felt something wet hit my forehead, and I looked up to see a few tears fall from Dez's eyes.

"I'm sorry. Karter, don't leave me over this. I'll hire somebody to take over at the daycare. I'm fucked up about us losing our baby too, and I blame myself for that shit, but don't leave me." By now, we both had tears running down our faces as we stood in the middle of the living room. I pulled his face down to mine and kissed his lips. His hands went right down to my booty as he pulled me closer to him.

"Ok, don't start nothing in here, Dez."

"Can you do that now?"

"I mean, I could, but we're not about to go there any time soon."

"Like, how long you talking about, bae?"

I laughed and sat down on the couch. "Until I say so, is that a problem?"

"Naw, man." He huffed and flopped down on the couch next to me.

"You are a big baby, Dezmund."

"That's cool. I'm yo big baby, though."

Melodee

I had been working overtime to get stuff together for the opening of the club. When Karter lost her baby, I pushed the date back to open the Saturday before Halloween. I posted that it was going to be a 90's party, so hopefully, all these hoes didn't show up as Aaliyah.

I was doing a last-minute check of the club to make sure everything was set up perfectly, and I called Karter to see if she was coming.

"Hey, Melly Mel."

"Hey boo, you sound all happy, what you doing?"

"I am happy. I been staring at this trophy all day." Her team had won the captain solo and creative dance last week, and that's all she'd been talking about. I was proud of all the girls.

"You coming tonight, riiiight?"

"Yes, girl. I'm coming, for the hundredth time."

"I was making sure, you know you like to send people off and claim you was reading or something."

"For your information, I have been reading, but I'm coming for real. I even talked Dez into dressing like Andre 3000, so I can be Erykah Badu."

"Y'all so lame, ugh. Well ok, I'll see you tonight, you drinking?"

"I don't know, Dez was talking about he not babysitting me, so I doubt it."

"Good, cuz I ain't babysitting yo ass either."

"Bye, hoe."

She hung up, and I finished my walkthrough. Everything was exactly how I wanted, so I was going home to take a quick nap.

When I got to Dame's house, he was standing in front of me with some Chipotle.

"Thank you, I was just thinking about Chipotle."

"Yeah, I know, you taking a nap with me?"

"Hell yeah, I'm tired."

I ate my food, then took a shower before I set my alarm and took a nap. I had to be up and the club by eight so I could unlock the liquor for the bartender, and I wasn't leaving until I closed the door.

When my alarm went off, Dame had to wake me up three more times, because I kept going back to sleep. Now, I was running late and had to rush.

I was dressed up like Left Eye and had my hair in big bantu knots. Dame was acting like a female getting ready, so I was waiting on him.

"Dame, I'm gon' leave without you, hurry up."

"Maaannn, chill out. I'm always waiting on yo ass." He came out the guest room, and I started dying laughing. He had on an Jheri curl wig with a Raiders hat, and a Raiders jersey.

"Who are you supposed to be, Damien?"

"Fuck you laughing for? I'm Ice Cube, nigga."

"Naahhh, you just messed my man all the way up."

"You a hater, bro. Come on."

We rode to the club, and I was recording Dame on Snapchat as he imitated Ice Cube. I always had fun when I was with Dame because we both were silly, and played all day.

The line to get into the club was wrapped around the corner, and we opened the doors 30 minutes earlier. When I saw Dez and Karter, I think I laughed harder than what I did with Dame. Karter actually got Dez's always serious ass to dress up.

"Mel, if yo ass say anything funny, I'm firing yo ass."

"Damn, you being petty like that, bro? It's cool. Y'all look good, though."

We were all sitting in our private section when Jazz came waltzing in and sat next to Dez and Karter.

"Hey, you guys."

'Can we help you?"

"I thought we were ok now, Karter?"

"You need to go, Jazz." Dez rubbed Karter's thigh, and I could tell it took a lot for her to stay calm."

"I just came up here because I don't know anyone else, but clearly you're still a little salty about everything. I'm sorry if you feel a little threatened, but I don't want him."

Crash!

Boom!

"Karter!"

"What the hell going on in here?"

Destini walked into the section to witness Karter beating Jazz's ass — just like I said she was. Dez let it go on for about a good three minutes before he picked Karter up and carried her toward his office.

"Sis got hands! Jazz, you better get yo ass up before my girl be tagging you next."

"Damn, she is cute, though. I can't have no bitch that can't fight, though. If some shit pop off and we out together, it's a wrap; her ass can't help."

We all started laughing as Jazz struggled to get up and walk herself outside. "I ain't never seen Karter act a fool like that; she was always so sweet and innocent."

"That's the problem. People like to underestimate my best friend, then she gotta make an example outta some hoes."

"She probably upstairs throwing hands at Dez. I should go check on my brother, man."

"Destini, you better sit down, where yo girl at?"

"Around this bitch somewhere, I don't know."

"Ugh, you worse than yo brothers. Why are y'all so rude?"

"Ain't nobody rude."

"Yeah, whatever."

Karter and Dez came back to the section, and she was smiling like nothing ever happened.

"Bae, tell somebody come clean this up. I don't want to slip. Hey, Destini. I ain't know you was here."

"Yeah, I saw yo whole MMA fight. You bet not be putting yo hands on bro."

"Shut up, I don't put my hands on nobody. That skeezer has been testing me. I had to give her what she was looking for."

"Man, when is the wedding? Fuck all that other shit, I'm ready to celebrate this black love. And I'm wearing a suit! Y'all know Ma gon' spazz if y'all don't come to the house tomorrow?"

"We'll be there, I already talked to her."

The rest of the night went smooth, and we were actually able to party all night — until we got shut down for the night for being over capacity. It was such a live night. Dez agreed to open back up regularly and let me handle most of the work. I already had plan to get a permanent stage added for Karaoke night and everything.

Dame kept telling me how proud he was, and it felt good to hear it from someone other than Karter. I can admit, Karter wasn't the only person who fell in love with the King of Chicago; one of them, anyway.

Dezmund "Dez"

It had been a few Sundays since we all came to Ma's house; so today, we were up at nine in the morning getting dressed. Karter acted like she had been drinking all night the way she was dragging her feet around the room.

"I'm so sore, bae. I just want to stay in the bed all day. But, I want some food, and I don't wanna get cussed out."

"That's what yo ass get for fighting and shit, but I was 'bout two seconds from flexing her ass myself, though, no lie. Or getting Destini to do it."

"Yeah, whatever. That bitch just better not show her face nowhere near me, or that's what she gon' be getting every time I see her ass. I can't believe she had the nerve to say I'm salty. Are you sure nothing happened between y'all?"

"Bae, come on now. We moved past this already. We not going back, love."

"I know, I just don't want nothing popping up out the blue."

"We good, Bugs, now come on before we be too late and Melodee and Dez eat all the damn food."

"Oh my God, I forgot they was gon' be there." She started rushing around, making sure she had everything while I sat downstairs waiting for her.

We drove to Ma's house, and Karter was singing and dancing the whole ride there. It was good to see her finally happy again. After we lost the baby, I don't think she smiled for a few weeks; all she did was stay in the bed.

"Finally, y'all got here. Ma being petty, talking about we got to wait for her baby, Karter." Destini opened the door, and we walked in and went straight to the kitchen.

"Hey Ma, it's smelling good as hell in here. Ow!"

"Watch yo mouth on my Father's day. You ain't too old to get yo butt whooped, Dezmund."

"Hey, Ma." Karter gave my mom a hug, and it was like she didn't want to let her go.

"How you feeling, baby? I been worried about you. I ain't gon' fuss at you for not answering the phone, but if you do it again, I will be at y'alls doorstep. What y'all kids say about pulling off?"

"It's pull up, Ma. Tell her yo pull up game strong."

"Destini, don't be teaching my mama that sh— stuff."

We all gathered around the dining room table, and Ma led us in prayer before everyone dug into their food.

"So, when is this wedding? I'm ready to get my good hat out. Karter, I could've let you wear my old dress, but you ain't got enough breasts to fit it." Melodee started laughing, and Karter stuck her middle finger up when Ma wasn't looking.

"I saw that, Karter."

"Sorry, Ma."

"How do you feel about trying for another baby? I need me some grandbabies around here, I get lonely. I'm tired of seeing Destini's freeloading behind at my door."

"Dang, Ma, that's how you treat your favorite?"

"Who the hell—oohh, forgive me. Who lied and told you that you was my favorite?" Dame and I started laughing, until Ma gave us that look we used to get right before she smacked us.

"I don't like neither one of y'all, if we being honest, shoot."

"Aite, remember that when you need to go to Target or something."

"And you gon' bring yo ass over here and take me."

"I'll take you, Ma. I'm always in Target anyway. And, to answer your question, I do want to try for another baby. I want a big family." I smiled at Karter because this was the first time I ever heard her say that. Whenever I asked, she would just say she didn't know, or she'd just change the subject.

"Well good, don't let what happened discourage you from trying again. Just release all those negative thoughts, and put your trust in the Lord. Before you know it, I'll have ten grandbabies running around. Melodee, I don't know what you over there snickering for. I know y'all not gon' be too far behind them."

"Naw, Ma. I gotta disagree on that one. This here birth control in my arm protects me for three more years, won't catch me slipping."

We finished eating, and as always, the women cleared the table and had me and Dame wash the dishes. When everything was clean, I walked into the living room with everyone else, and saw Karter was sleep already.

"Take her to yo old room, and don't be doing no nasty stuff in my house, Dezmund. I'll kick that door open swinging my belt."

"I thought you said you wanted some grandbabies?"

"Don't test me, Dezmund. I keep telling y'all kids you ain't too old to catch these hands."

"I'm playing, Ma, dang. And stop listening to stuff yo daughter be saying. Talking about catch these hands." I shook my head and carried Karter to my old room. I was about to walk out when her voice stopped me.

"Bae, come lay with me."

"What's on yo mind, love?"

"Let's just get married without the big wedding. It's only gon' be six people there anyway, we don't have to go all out."

"Are you sure that's what you want?"

"Yeah, maybe in a few years, I'll have more friends and we can celebrate then."

"Ok Queen, you can have whatever you want. You the one that's gon' tell Ma she can't wear her good hat, though."

She laughed and laid on my chest. "I love you, Dez."

"Love you too, Bugs."

I ended up falling asleep with her and when we woke up, it was dark outside. All I heard was Melodee's loud mouth downstairs, yelling that Destini was cheating.

"Bout time y'all woke up. We was about to eat without y'all. Well, I know I wasn't about to wait no longer. Karter, you tryna get in on this card game?"

"I ain't playing no Uno, though. Last time, Destini's ass cheated the whole time."

"I told you!"

"Ain't nobody cheat, y'all just suck. We can get the regular cards so me and Dame can bust y'all in Spades."

"Um, Dame is my partner. You can try again, though."

"Nah bae, you don't know how to play. I'll have to teach you at home or something."

"You petty, you supposed to have my back."

We stayed at Ma's house until she put us out around ten o'clock. It was times like this that made my decision to step away from the street easy. Ain't no way I would've brought Karter into that shit. I mean, yeah, I had to catch a body because of her ex. But, that was the last of that, unless I absolutely had to.

Monday morning, I went to go over applications for someone to take over at the daycare full-time. There was a knock at my office door, and Jazz walked in.

"Bro, what the fuck is up with you? You like getting yo ass beat? Cuz that's what gon' happen if my wife see you in here."

"I just came to find out what's really going on? I got attacked for no reason, and no one did anything to help me."

"Fuck you want me to do about that?"

"Don't worry, I'll just have the law take care of it. I know there's cameras everywhere in your little club."

I stood up and had to sit back down in my seat before I choked the snot out of her ass.

"I see that got your attention."

"What you want, man?"

"You gotta let me sample that dick, and I'll leave you alone."

"Bitch, you sound crazy as hell, you better take this money and get the fuck on."

"I'll give you some time to think about it. You got until my eye goes down to give me your answer." She switched out of my office, and I was on ten.

"Wassup, bro?"

"Destini, come to the daycare. like right now."

"I ain't watching them bad ass kids, bro. I did that shit one time and was ready to fight them, and their parents."

"Just bring yo ass on, and hurry up." I hung up and went outside so I could smoke.

Destini showed up when I was sparking my second blunt. "Damn bro, what's going on?"

"I need you to take care of Jazz for me. Bitch call herself threatening to go to the police and press charges on Karter."

"For getting beat up? Damn, hoes can't just take L's and move on no more? I got you."

Destini was our own personal hitta when we needed people taken care of, male or female, in this case.

I passed her the blunt, and she got in her car to leave. I went to my office and thought about the shit I had to deal with. It's like when me and Karter's relationship started getting better, some shit popped up that could ruin us. This time, I was getting ahead of the shit, and Jazz had me fucked up if she thought I was gon; fuck her. I admit, if I was single, I would've ran through her and on my way, but I wasn't built like that.

I scheduled some interviews for tomorrow, and I was gon' make Karter come with me so we wouldn't have no more problems.

When I made it home, Karter was gone, so I called to check on her.

"Hello?"

"Where you at, bae?"

"I had some runs to make, where you at?"

"Shiiittt, at home looking for my future wife."

"Well, I'll be back after I go check the mail at my house. Can you take something out for me to cook?"

"How 'bout we just go out? It's been a while since we both was free for a night."

"Ok, I'll see you when I get home."

Karter

I was out shopping for a Christmas present for Dez, and I didn't know what to get somebody that basically had everything.

"Girl, you better put a bow on and say you his gift."

"I know you seen them videos on Facebook. I cannot gift something he get on the regular."

"But, you ain't let that man touch you in how long? You better stop playing and buss it open for a real nigga."

"Melodee, shut up, there's kids in here." We were in Target. I don't know what I was going to find, but I was gon' try.

"Well, they mammy better tell them don't be in grown folks' business."

"You will never be allowed to babysit my kids alone."

"Yeah right, you gon' be begging me to get them."

"I didn't tell Dez, but I'm terrified to get pregnant again. I keep thinking I'll lose another baby, and I think I'll lose my mind if that happens."

"You can't think like that, boo. We don't know why you lost the baby, but it don't mean it's going to happen again."

My phone rang, interrupting us, and it was a number I didn't recognize. "Hello, this is Karter."

"Hey Karter, this is Ms. Williams who stays next door to you. I was just calling to let you know there's been a couple that's been stopping by the house looking for you.

They're here now, looking through the window. I was getting ready to call the police, but I wanted to call you first."

"Thank you so much, Ms. Williams, I'm on my way now."

I hung up and grabbed my purse out of the cart I was pushing. I practically ran out the door, with Melodee right behind me.

"Girl, what the hell are we running for?"

"That was nosey ass Ms. Williams from next door. She said somebody's been coming to the house looking for me, and I want to see who it is."

Meet me at my house NOW!

Bet

I texted Dez and sped all the way home. When I made it, I saw a man and a woman standing in front of the house, and it look like they were arguing.

"I told you we should've waited until later, there's nobody here."

"Um, can I help you?" They turned around to look at me, and they both had shocked expressions on their face.

"Karter?"

"Yes, who are you?"

"We're your parents, you don't remember us?"

I stood, staring at them like they had an extra head. The last time I saw my "parents" was when they dropped me off at Big Mama's house.

"Mommy, where we going?"

"Just sit the hell back, Karter, damn. You ask too many questions." My father snapped at me and I was getting to cry, until we pulled up to Big Mama's house. I loved coming here because Big Mama would always make me fresh chocolate cookies.

"Gone head in there, tell her we running to the store."

"Ok Mommy, can you bring me something back?" Her eyes watered as I got out the car, and I grabbed my bag she had me pack.

My dad pulled off before I could even get to the front door, but I didn't think nothing about it.

"Karter? Why you standing out here by yourself, baby?"

"Daddy told me to tell you they were going to the store."

Big Mama shook her head and grabbed my bag from me.

I sat all night, waiting in the window, hoping my mother came back, but she never did.

"Big Mama, did I do something wrong?"

"No baby, some people just can't appreciate such wonderful people."

"Karter?" Dez's voice snapped me out of my thoughts, and I looked back to see him walking up to me, gripping his gun tight in his right hand.

"Woah, we didn't come to cause any trouble. I just wanted to come see you and Big Mama, but Ms. Williams told me she passed."

"What you coming to see me for?"

"Alright Karter, you're not going to disrespect your mother in front of me."

"Nigga, what mother? The only mother I knew died, so like I said before, what you coming to see me for?"

He took a step toward me, and Dez put his gun to his head. "I wish the fuck you would, homie."

I heard tires screeching, and Dame hopped out of his car with his gun in his hand too. "Fuck going on around here?"

"We're just going to leave, go Kevin." Kevin walked to the car, and my mother turned around looking at me with a sad face.

"Karter, I just want to say I'm sorry for everything. I know it'll take more than that, but I really want a relationship with you. I know I missed a lot already, but I want to make up for everything, if you'll let me." She dug in her purse for something, then pulled out a paper she wrote her number down on. Reluctantly, I took the paper and she got in the Buick that they came in.

"What the fuck just happened?"

"Shut up, Dame. Karter, call me later, boo."

"Ok."

They got in the car together, and I went into the house.

"You good, Karter?"

"No, how the fuck she just gon' pop up after 20 years, talking about she wants to make up? I'm grown as fuck, they should've came back from the store like they said they were. I spent years crying to Big Mama, asking why they didn't want me. I'm good on them."

"You sure you don't want to hear yo moms out?"

"I don't want to think about that right now."

My emotions were all over the place. On one hand, I wanted answers. I needed answers. For the first five years after they left, I honestly thought they were dead, and I stopped thinking about them all together. Now, I was wishing I still had Big Mama here to handle everything.

Dez waited with me while I went through the mail and paid the bills that were here.

"You wanna take a trip?"

"Where we going?"

"I don't know, bae, but we dealing with so much shit, we just need a vacation."

"That sounds good. I swear, I need it."

"Aite, come on."

"We're leaving right now?"

"Yeah, I ain't took a flight in a minute. You don't need to pack nothing, let's just go."

I was smiling hard as he led me out the house and to my truck. I got in the passenger side as he parked his car in the garage.

The ride to O'Hare Airport took almost an hour with the midday Chicago traffic, and I was acting like that impatient child who couldn't sit still.

"Where are we going, Dez?"

"Why you can't just go with the flow for once? I see what I gotta do for you, turn around." Dez took his tie off and covered my eyes.

"You better not run me into a wall, Dezmund."

"I got you, baby. Put the headphones in yo ear and play something loud."

"You're doing too much now, Dez."

"Put the damn headphones in yo ear, man."

I did what he said, and he held my hand and led me through the airport. Five minutes later, I was being led up some stairs and into a seat. I felt the plane taking off, and Dez took the bootleg blindfold off my eyes. My mouth dropped to the floor as I looked around. The plane we were in only had six seats in it, but it had a full setup that looked better than my living room. I took myself on a tour and found two bathrooms, an office, and a small kitchen. There was also a door that led to a bedroom, and there was a big California King bed in the middle of the room.

"How much did all this cost?"

"I got a good deal on it, don't worry about all that. It's paid for already."

"You ain't had none of yo old hoes in here, did you?"

"I ain't have hoes, baby girl."

"Whatever the hell you wanna call them, were they in here?"

"Nah, I just bought it earlier this year. I haven't even flown on it yet."

"You wanna break the bed in?"

"You dead ass?"

"Yeah, you better hurry up and take them clothes off."

"We got five hours, I got plenty of time."

He pulled my shirt over my head and lifted me up so I could wrap my legs around his waist.

"I'm putting a baby in you tonight."

Dez laid me down on the bed and ate my kitty until I was seeing stars. When I felt his manhood entering me for the first time in weeks, I swear I heard a choir singing.

I tapped out after the second round and fell asleep as soon as my head hit the pillow. I didn't wake up until I felt Dez carrying me back to the seats, and strapping me in my seat belt.

"We're getting ready to land. You drooling and shit, bae."

"Shut up." I wiped my face and stood up so we could get off the plane.

"Welcome to San Francisco, baby."

"Ooohhhh yes, bae! I'm about to spend all of your money, I need to get some new clothes."

"That's cool, I'll make it right back. You wanna nap, or you ready to get into some shit?"

"We need something to wear, Dez, what time is it? Do we got time to go to a store?"

"Calm down, bae, our car's already waiting. Let's go to the hotel first."

He bent down so I could get on his back, and he walked to a black Suburban that was waiting. We pulled up to the Fairmont hotel, and the driver opened our door.

"What time should I be back, sir?"

"Just come back tomorrow morning by 9 o'clock, enjoy your night."

Dez grabbed my hand and led me into the hotel. He got us checked in, and we got our room key. Our suite was huge and had a gorgeous view of the city and water. When I went to the bedroom, there were bags from different clothing and shoe stores spread all over the floor.

"Pick something. There should be dresses in the closet. We going downstairs to eat before we go to the club, so choose wisely."

I went to the closet, and my eyes landed on a red, off-the-shoulder bandage dress, and I knew that's what I was going to put on.

I took a shower and put my hair in a neat ponytail. My hair was done, but Dez messed it up on the plane. When I was dressed, I gave myself a long once over. I had no idea what he had planned for tonight, but I was "going with the flow," as he said.

"Bae, I'm surprised you're not wearing a suit."

"You tryna be funny, huh?"

"I'm just playing, you look good either way. I don't think I like those jeans, though."

"What's wrong with 'em?"

"I can see your print and if I can see it, then other people can see it too. I don't wanna have to smack no bitches for staring."

"If I catch a bitch staring, bae, I'll slap her myself."

"You play too much. I'm ready to eat, I hope this shit is good."

"Shiiiit, me too. I ain't ate since earlier, ya man is hungry."

"Well, come on."

We went downstairs to the restaurants and ate our food. The server recommended a club, so we ordered an Uber and went to go check it out. The club was packed, and the DJ was playing nice good. The drink was fye too; I had got so drunk from drinking Long Island Iced Teas all night that Dez had to carry me up to our room. We made love all night, and didn't stop until we got a call from the front desk about the noise.

I went to sleep with a smile on my face. This vacation was looking good already.

Jazmyne

"Are you freaking crazy? Why did you say you was going to the police, Jazz?"

I was at home on the phone with my best friend, Chloe.

"I panicked, I didn't know what else to do. But, if you see what that crazy bitch did to my face, you'll be saying the same."

"Jazz, you always get yourself into some shit, and I'm sorry, but I can't get in the middle of it this time."

"Wow, some best friend you are."

"I am a great best friend, that's why I'm here to tell you you're fucking up. Just pack your shit and come on back home."

"Fine, I'll see you later tonight." I hung up and went to pack all my clothes.

Let me introduce myself. I'm Jazmyne Fields, born and raised in Indianapolis, Indiana, but I moved to Chicago a little over a year ago, looking for my next hustle. When I saw Dez at the mall, all I saw was dollar signs and when I did my research on him, I knew I had to get him. The night he showed up at my house in the middle of the night, I just knew I was going to trap him, but he passed out on me and was too heavy for me to try to move.

When I got done packing everything up, it was dark outside, so I decided I wasn't gon' hit the road until morning time.

As I was warming up my food from earlier, all my power went out.

"What the hell?" I looked out the window, and all my neighbors' lights were on. I went to my bedroom to get my cellphone when I heard a noise like someone came in the door.

"Hello?" My heart was beating fast as I ran and grabbed my cellphone off the bed.

"Put it down."

Click

The sound of a gun had me throwing my hands up.

"Please don't kill me, I promise I was leaving town, you don't have to do this."

I heard a whistling song, and felt a sharp pain in my back.

The feeling of that first bullet entering my body sent me into shock, so I didn't even feel the second one.

I was laid face down on the rug in my room, and I heard the whoever it was who just shot me running down the stairs and out the house. I start looking around for my phone, and it was under the bed. I reached out to get it, and the pain in my back had me screaming loud.

"OOOOWWWWW!! Oh my God, I need help!" I grabbed my phone and went to my last call; it was Chloe.

"Hey boo, you on your way? Jazz? Did you butt dial me again?"

"Help me." I finally got my voice out, and I heard Chloe gasp loudly.

"Where are you, Jazz? What happened? I'm calling 911 on my house phone, don't hang up. Talk to me, Jazz."

"I'm at home. I think Karter shot me. I'm dying, bestie, it's hard to breathe."

I heard Chloe crying and talking to the dispatcher. I was in and out of consciousness, and I started seeing white lights everywhere. All the shady shit I did to people over the years, I knew I wasn't going to Heaven, but I was still praying I did.

"I'm sorry for everything, Chloe. I know I did a lot of terrible things to you, and I'm so sorry, you're the only person that was always there for me."

"Don't talk like that, Jazz. You're going to be ok, the ambulance is on the way."

I heard the sirens, but I knew they weren't going to get to me in time, especially with my front door locked.

"They're outside, Jazz, just hold on."

I heard my best friend talking to me, but I couldn't find my voice. I took my last breath lying on my bedroom floor, alone.

Dezmund "Dez"

Baby while we're young we should just have fun. We should just do whatever we want

And tell everyone that we fell in love with each other

Ooh, that we found the one in one another.

-Jhene Aiko

While we were in California, I had Melodee, Destini, and Dame getting our wedding together. I knew exactly what I wanted and how I wanted it, so all they had to do was put everything together. I was nervous as hell, but I was ready to make Karter my wife, so I had to suck that shit up. We had just landed at O'Hare, and my hands were shaking the whole walk to the parking garage.

"Bae, are you feeling ok?"

"Yeah, why you ask me that?"

"You look pale as hell, Dez, that's why." She was being dramatic, feeling my head to see if I had a fever, I guess.

I was riding around, trying to kill time until Dame let me know it was ok to come home, and Karter's face was twisted up as she looked around.

"Where are we going, Dez? I'm ready to get back in the bed."

"Just ride with me, bae."

"Can we ride later? It's nine in the morning, Dez. I don't see why you had me up in the middle of the night getting on a freaking plane anyway."

"Karter, I swear you'll fuck up a wet dream with all the questions you be asking, man." She sat with her arms folded across her chest.

I pulled into the gate and parked in front of the door.

"Karter?"

"Hmmm?"

"You love me, right?"

"Yeah, I love you, Dezmund. Why what did you do?"

"Nothing, you ready to be my wife?"

Melodee opened the door holding a dress, and Karter looked at me with her eyes big. She hopped out the truck and went into the house. All the furniture in the living room was gone, and there were chairs and an altar set up.

"I can't believe you did this, who are all these chairs for?"

"Girl, come get dressed, you ask too many questions."

"I told her ass that, bro. She wanted to get mad when I said it, though." Melodee pulled Karter to the master bedroom, and I went to one of the guest rooms. I got dressed in my navy-blue tuxedo and Ferragamo loafers, and stood in the mirror rehearsing my vows.

knock

knock

"Come in!"

Dame and Destini came in the room wearing matching suits, and I gave them both dap. "Thank y'all for coming through for me, I owe you big."

"You know we got you, bro. You sure you ready for this?"

"Yeah, I'm sure. Did you handle that other thing for me, though?"

"Yeah, you know I always get the job done."

"Good shit. Now, which one of y'all got me one rolled already?" They both pulled a pre- rolled blunt out, and I opened the window so we could smoke.

"I know y'all ain't in here getting lit without me." Melodee came in and took the blunt from Destini's mouth.

"You looking good, baby."

"Yeah, I know. Don't get no ideas over there, though."

"You supposed to be in there with my wife, why you in here?"

"Aw yeah, I almost forgot. She's ready, soooo go get in place, and I'm taking this with me."

"Bro, yo girl steal all damn day. It probably be all kind of shit missing in the crib."

I fixed my tux in the mirror one more time before I walked out to take my place at the altar, and Ma was sitting front row with tears in her eyes. There were about 40 people here, including some of the parents from her dance studio, and some of my mom's family who I hadn't seen in a few years.

Tevin Campbell's 'You', started playing, and everyone turned to face the stairway where Karter was coming from.

Melodee picked her wedding gown out, and she was looking good as hell in this navy blue, lace gown. Melodee walked her down the aisle and when she reached me, I lifted her veil and gave her a kiss on the lips.

"Y'all not at that part of the ceremony yet, bro. Relax." Destini spoke up, making everybody laugh.

I got back in place, and the minister started his opening remarks. "Dearly Beloved, we are here today to share with Dez and Karter, an important moment in their lives."

As he spoke, I stared deeply into Karter's eyes to see if I saw even a little bit of doubt, and thankfully, I didn't. I knew since the first time I saw Karter that she was going to be my wife. I didn't care that we had only been together for a few months; when you know, you just know.

"Please repeat after me. I, Dez, take you, Karter, to be my wife, my partner in life and my one true love. I will cherish our union, and love you more each day than I did the day before. I will trust you and respect you, laugh with you and cry with you, loving you faithfully through good times and bad, regardless of the obstacles we might face together. I give you my hand, my heart, and my love, from this day forward, as long as we both shall live."

Next, it was Karter's turn to repeat after him, but she was crying so hard, she could barely get her words out.

We exchanged rings, and I wiped the tears from Karter's face.

"By the power vested in me by the State of Illinois, I now pronounce you husband and wife. Now is the part where you can kiss your bride. I present to you, Mr. and Mrs. Wright." Everyone was on their feet clapping as we turned around to face them. We went to change into the outfit we were wearing to the reception, and I was throwing shit everywhere so that I could hurry up and get back to her.

It was a cold November, so I put on my Salute crewneck and jeans that Karter ordered from Black Pyramid. Her ass shopped too much, but at least she ordered shit for me too.

I walked back out, and everyone was loading up in tour buses we rented to transport everyone to the venue. A door opened from behind me, and Karter stepped out the room wearing the same crew neck as me, with some blue distressed jeans and her Ugg boats.

"Did you plan us to dress alike too?"

"Naw, great minds think alike."

"Yeah, you right."

We walked out the house, and I locked up, and helped Karter onto the bus that had Bride and Groom on it. I couldn't wait to go turn up at the reception, I needed a fat blunt and some Hennessy —we was making us a baby tonight!

Karter

I had officially been Mrs. Wright for three months now, and I was on cloud nine. I agreed to clear Big Mama's house out and rent it out. Dez had people come and do some work on the house, and I was on my way to go see the finished product. When I pulled up, I seen my mother sitting on the porch, and she had a black eye that looked fresh. It wasn't really cold at the end of March, but it was definitely too cold to just be sitting on the porch.

"How long have you been sitting out here? And what happened to your eye?"

"I been here all night. I didn't know you moved out, I was waiting and hoping you stopped by."

"Ok, so what happened to your eye?"

"Your father, he—"

"That's not my father."

"Well, Kevin, he beat my ass because I wouldn't agree to set you and your boyfriend up. He started smoking more, and he lost all our money gambling. He said your guy looked like he had money, and he wanted to rob him."

"Well, first of all, my HUSBAND would kill you and him if you even thought about it, and so would I. So, I advise you to leave, like now."

"I told him I wouldn't do it, and he snapped. I really came back to build a relationship with you. I'm sorry I let a man keep me away from you so long, but please Karter, you have to forgive me."

"I don't have to do shit but stay black and die. You really have to go; do you need some money?"

"I didn't come here for that, I don't want your money."

"Well, that's all I got for you, so here." I reached in and grabbed all the cash I had in my purse. "This should be enough to get you a room or a bus ticket, but don't come back here."

I walked past her and went into the house, making sure I locked the door behind me. When I looked around at Big Mama's house, completely empty, I broke down a little. I couldn't believe I was actually doing this. I always said I was never leaving this house. I was doing a full background and credit check on whoever I rent to, because if they messed this house up, I was going to be in jail for a homicide.

I wiped my tears and did my walkthrough of the house. I can't lie, this shit was nice. I was thinking about changing my mind again, but I ain't wanna hear Dezmund's mouth. When I left out, thankfully, my mother was gone, so I got in the car and headed to the studio for practice with the Divas.

I had a lot of new girls on both squads, and I was happy that people liked us enough to want to join the family.

There weren't any competitions I was signing us up for anytime soon, because I needed all of girls to be in sync with each other.

We worked on two stands that took us almost four hours to get it right. I called Dez after I dismissed all the girls, because he hated when I left out alone when it was dark.

"I'm pulling up now, baby."

"Ok."

I grabbed my bag and waited for him to knock on the door before I came out.

"You look tired as hell, bae."

"I am tired, you know I been running around, and I went to go look at the house."

He walked me around the building where my car was parked, and someone jumped out from behind the dumpster and scared me. Dez pulled me behind him, and the masked man was holding a gun to him.

"Give me your money!"

"Nigga, I ain't got no cash on me, fuck I look like?"

"Give me that watch then."

"Yeah, you can have it, I hope you let God see it too, bro."

Dez start playing with his watch, and I saw the gun that was tucked behind his back. I snatched it out and shot through the space Dez had between his arm. I wasn't looking, so I didn't even know if I shot him until I heard his body drop, and some groaning.

"Good shit, bae. Next time, I'mma need you to have your eyes open when you shoot."

He walked up to the man and bent down to take the mask off.

"Ain't this yo pops, bae?" I didn't say anything as I just stared at Kevin's chest move up and down slowly. I heard some sirens, and Dez stood up and dusted his pants off.

"Karter, come on, we gotta go."

"Did I...did I kill 'im?"

"It was either them or me, baby, but we can't sit here and discuss this shit right now."

My ears were still ringing from the gunshot, and my head was spinning. I just knew I was going to pass out, until Dez grabbed my arm and had to basically dragging me to the car. I was still holding the smoking gun as Dez drove like a bat outta hell. I didn't think I would get that visual out of my head of that body hitting the ground. I never even shot a gun before. *God, I hope I don't get punished for this.*

"Shit!"

"What?"

I snapped out of my trance to see blue lights flashing behind us. I started to panic, but Dez took the gun and stashed it in a secret compartment that was in the dash.

"Just relax, bae, I'll take care of this, it's probably because I was speeding."

I saw his lips moving, but I couldn't hear anything over the sound of my racing heart.

Dez rolled the window down halfway as one officer came to his window, and another was on the passenger side flashing his light in my face.

"License, registration, and proof of insurance, please?"

"What am I being stopped for, Officer?"

"You were going 80 in a 65, sir."

"Aite bro, I gotta reach in the glove compartment."

"Move slowly." The officer had his hand on his gun, and my eyes got big as I watched his every move. With all the shit going on with police killing black people, males especially, I feared for Dez's life as well as my own.

Dez handed over his documents, and the officers walked back to their car. Five minutes later, another squad car pulled up, and Dez cursed under his breath as they approached the car again. This time, the officer tapped on my window.

"Ma'am, do you have identification?"

"What you need her shit for? I'm the one driving, you pulled me over for speeding, right? Fuck outta here with that shit."

"Babe, it's ok, calm down." I got my license and handed it to the officer. He stepped back and said something into his walkie talkie before he came back to my window.

"Ma'am, I need you to step out and put your hands behind your back."

"Karter, don't get yo ass out this car." Dez rolled my window back up and the officer snatched at the door handle. I didn't know what to do as I felt the urge to throw up all over the place.

"You bet not fuck my door up while you snatching on my shit." The officer put his hand on his gun, but this time, he pulled it out and had it pointing at me.

"Open the door and step out, NOW!"

"Get your fucking gun out my wife face, bitch." Dez hopped out the car and sprinted around the car, and I got out too so I could stop him from doing something crazy.

"Dezmund, NO! Get back in the car, please, just get back in the car." The officer grabbed my arm and threw me against the car, and the next thing I knew, Dez punched him in the face and he hit the ground. Another squad car pulled up, and I tried to grab my phone off the seat so I could call Melodee or Dame, or anybody.

"PUT YOUR HANDS UP, NOW!"

We now had five guns drawn on us, and Dez just gave me a hug and kissed me on the lips.

"Don't say shit, whatever they ask you, ok? You. Don't. Know. Shit." I shook my head up and down, and he gave me a kiss on the lips.

Dez put his hands up and got down on his knees, so I did the same thing.

He was tackled first and put into handcuffs, then they grabbed me. As I was put into the back of a police car, I was crying my eyes out. When we made it to the station, I was put in a cold room and handcuffed to a chair. I think I was sitting there for an hour, and the whole time, I heard Dez yelling that they better not had touch me.

A female officer dressed in a pantsuit walked into the room with a file in her hand, and she sat down in front of me.

"Hello, Mrs. Wright. I'm Detective Normal, and I'm investigating the murder of a Ms. Jazmyne Fields."

"What? And what does that have to do with me?"

"We have suspicion to believe you had something to do with it, or at least know something about it. I'm just trying to get to the bottom of this."

"I don't know anything about that, I didn't even know she was dead. So you can get me a lawyer if I'm being accused of something so serious."

Here I was, thinking I was arrested for shooting my father, and it was about Jazz. I honestly didn't know she was killed. I wondered if Dez had something to do with that.

"Is that your final answer?"

"Yes, it is. I'll take lawyer for eight hundred, Alex."

"Ok, I see we have a regular old comedian on our hands. Take a look at these pictures and I'll be back."

She left out the room and left me sitting in the room by myself. I looked down at the pictures, and they were of Jazz laying on the floor, with blood all over the front of her shirt. I pushed the pictures onto the floor.

Another detective came in and sat in the same chair Detective Normal was previously in.

"How are you, Mrs. Wright?"

"I'll be fine when I can get out of here. Can I get my phone call, please?"

"Yeah, I can help you out if you can help me out."

"I don't know how I can help you, sir. Where is my husband?"

"Your husband is fine, it's you I'm worried about. Do you know how serious it is to be looked at for a homicide? It's looking premeditated in the eyes of the law. If I understand correctly, Ms. Fields had an affair with your husband?"

"Noooo, she didn't have shit with my husband, so you don't understand correctly, obviously."

"We have a witness that says you two got into an altercation at your husband's club, the day before she got killed, is that correct?"

"Well, I don't know when she got killed. But I could've sworn I asked for a lawyer, why are you even in here?" He gave me slick smile and stood up out the chair. "We'll be back with you shortly."

After what felt like an eternity of sitting in this room alone, I started to get pissed, and I had to pee. All I could think about was Dez, and that they were going to do something to him. I hadn't heard his voice in an hour, and I was wondering if he was even still in the precinct.

"HEELLLLLOOOOOO!! I NEED TO GO TO THE BATHROOM! CAN ANYBODY HEAR ME?" I started banging on the table with my free hand, and someone finally opened the door.

"Can I help you?" This six-foot lady came in here with an attitude, like I wanted to be in here.

"Somebody need to help me, I have to use the bathroom. I been sitting here for hours, when can I make my phone call? And, where the hell is my husband and my lawyer for the 50th time? I'm going to sue the shit out of the city."

"They actually told me to come let you go, so come on, you can follow me. But, make sure you keep your phone on, and don't leave the country anytime soon." She unlocked the cuffs, and I had to move my hand around to get feeling back in them. I stood up to walk in front of her when she gently grabbed my arm.

"Ma'am, did you get hurt?"

"No, why?"

"There's blood on your pants."

I looked down, and sure enough, there was blood between my legs. I didn't know what the hell was going on because I had my period already, at least I thought I did. I actually couldn't remember when the last time I had my period.

"Oh my God, I need to get to a hospital." I ran out the room and saw Dame and Melodee standing in the waiting room looking pissed.

"Mel, take me to the hospital, where is Dez, has he come out already?"

"They not tryna let him go, talking about because he assaulted a police officer. What happened, did they hurt you?"

"No, I'm bleeding. What do you mean they're not letting him go? They can't just hold him here, can they? The officer had thrown me against the car, and y'all know how Dez gets."

"Our lawyer is here. He'll be straight, sis. Let's go get you checked out to make sure you're ok."

Melodee pulled me out the door, and Dame was trailing right behind us. She got in the backseat with me, and I started to cry in my lap.

"What if I'm losing another baby, Mel? Now, my husband is in jail and they think I killed Jazz. My life is going from sugar to shit so fast."

"What?!" Dame and Melodee yelled at the same time, and Dame looked back at me with a strange face, like he knew something I didn't.

"When did she get killed?"

"I don't know, I thought the bitch just finally found her some business. They said the day after I whooped her ass in the club, but I didn't do the shit."

"Just relax, we know you're innocent. They don't have any evidence, that's why they couldn't hold you in there."

Dame's phone rang, and he handed it to me.

"Here, it's bro."

"Hello?"

"Baby, you good?"

"No, I'm bleeding, Dez. I think I'm losing another baby, I'm so scared. Where are you? Are you ok?"

"Calm down, I'll be there soon, ok?"

"When is soon?"

"I don't know, bae. I can't lie, I might do a little time because I'm about to knock a few more of they asses out up in here."

"Dezmund, stop." I laughed, and he did too.

"I just wanted to hear you laugh, I gotta go, but I'mma see you soon. Don't be stressing my baby out in there, aite? I love you, Queen."

"I love you too, King."

To Be Continued....

Have You Read These Yet?

#Free With Kindle Unlmited!

79408387R00133

Made in the USA
Lexington, KY
21 January 2018